NEW CHRISTIAN PARABLES

Part 2
The Lawyer's Lullaby & A Maze in Grace
Written By Jwyan C. Johnson

Take a sip of the "bible study smoothie:" designed for anyone to memorize scriptures to the rhythm of mystery-laced morals, with the symbolism of today. Learn how faith works in *The Parable of Ice-Cream Soup!* Awaken pride with *The Lawyer's Lullaby Parable.* And inspire anyone with *The Parable of the Calendar's Watch!* Experience plenty more parables, and a bonus of *Character Commentaries* and *Family Skits*, its "wordplay" in more ways than one! Fill your "thirsty cup" to the top!

The **Story** Version

The **WordPlay®** Version

The **Family Skit** Version

ISBN: 978-0615976969 Image Reflections Publishing

Example: The Importance of Bible Study
The Thirsty Cup Parable
To reach the top of the water fountain, the thirsty schoolboys work together.

Included with this parable:
- Story Symbolism
- Moral of the Story
- Fun Facts & Discussion Questions
- *Instant Replay* Bible Study

Simply <u>choose</u> your version of choice for this parable below:

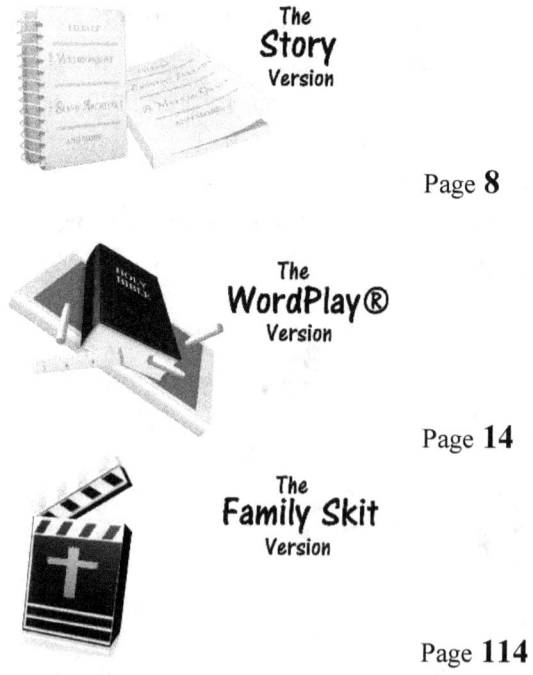

The
Story
Version

Page **8**

The
WordPlay®
Version

Page **14**

The
Family Skit
Version

Page **114**

Preface
The Alphabetical Chase

Years ago, award-winning author Jwyan C. Johnson wrote the script to a cartoon. The story starts off with a police chase to a giant dictionary: the home of our vocabulary words. Cops break down the cover, and they all rush in with their weapons drawn. And as they move around inside this book, we learn that they're looking for one specific word: a simple 9-lettered noun. It has been bragging about its countless offenses committed against our society, against mankind. Surprising unarmed, and not dangerous, this specific word simply turns us against each other.

Detectives follow the "alphabetical" directions to the right page, the right column and the right row, only to discover that this word has disappeared! Nowadays this divisive word lives inside our minds if we let it! The accomplished mystery writer reveals that "ignorance" was the word the police were after.

WordPlay Christian Parables 2 joins the creative aim to biblically "protect and serve" the mind state. Ignorance is still at large in our society! But there are some places where ignorance no longer resides so we can win back each other. So are you ready? Let's break some barriers together.

Table of Contents

The Story Version   The WordPlay® Version   The Family Skit Version

---

A Maze In Grace (The Parable)
It's the most popular 3-D maze challenge for Little Gracie.

Story 16   WordPlay 64   Family Skit 120

The Parable of Ice-Cream Soup
A little girl learns about the conditions of Faith in an unlikely place.

Story 21   WordPlay 69   Family Skit 134

The Parable of the Lawyer's Lullaby
A determined lawyer hires a Detective to solve a mystery around the courtroom conditions against her last case.

Story 24   WordPlay 72   Family Skit 139

Peculiar Treasure (The Parable) (Poetry)

An 'enchanted wish' comes true in the 'closest' of ways!

Batteries Not Included (The Parable)

Jeffrey learns the difference between the game he is playing, and "the game he was playing!"

The Parable of the Waitress's Tip

A mysteriously absent waitress adds insight to the menu for a starving customer.

The Parable of the Counselor's Gift

A school counselor gains exaggerated popularity amongst a curious news reporter, despite a statistical mystery.

The Parable of the Calendar's Watch

A "familiar" celebrity is asked to help promote a mysterious product.

Couples Therapy Parable (Poetry)

"…as their Exes cheer against them…"

The Parable of The Blindfold

A patient sneaks to another doctor for a second opinion.

The Blindfold Parable 2: Testing Faith

Faith is tested thoroughly in an impromptu patient's visit.

Visit Us!

Join our mailing list to receive updates, teaching materials, and new upcoming parables!

www.ChristianParables.com

Image Reflections Publishing
Copyright ©2014 All rights reserved.
ISBN: 978-0615976969
Jwyan C. Johnson has granted its syndicates and affiliates non-exclusive displaying rights.

**The
Story
Version**

The Importance of Bible Study

The Thirsty Cup Parable

To reach the top of the water fountain, the thirsty schoolboys work together.

"I'll lift you on the count-uh three," Frank tells Christian.

"One…" they say together, "Two… THREE!" Frank holds his friend Christian up, with all his child strength, and can hear the water now flowing.

"Hurry up Christian," Frank says as the seconds get heavier. "Is our cup almost full?"

"What cup?" Christian replies puzzled.

"The big cup we got from the cafeteria! We can save it for later. You're not even thirsty right now!"

"Yeah but this way, I will continue to feel full."

"Forget using your mouth to feel full! Use your cup for a full fill!"

Christian's 'weight' becomes too much for Frank to hold, causing them both to fall.

"Sorry Frank!"

As Christian tries to return the favor, he simple isn't strong enough to lift his friend up.

The End

Story Symbolism

- Cafeteria = Wisdom
- Christian = Christians
- Fountain = Bible
- Lift = Support
- Water = Scriptures
- Cup = Heart
- Drink = Experience
- Thirsty = Troubled

Moral

Frank(ly) to every Christian, how can a "cup runneth over" if we drink directly from the faucet? Wisdom is feeling (and filling) The Word in your heart (both are needed) so you'll never urgently "thirst" for biblical instruction.

Character Interaction

The good news, for both Christian and Frank, is the sound of their much taller friend walking down that same hall. And that person is you! Can you them fill their cup? Can you store 20 scriptures? Take *Christian's Challenge!* Learn how on Chapter 4

Chapter 1

Tips When Sharing a Parable

Reach or Teach? - From *WordPlay Christian Parables* Book 1

Tell me which word comes first in the dictionary: "reach" or "teach?" An alphabetically fitting experience: we must reach first and teach later. To skip the reach (out) first is to appear redundant and cloned at times: not the most attractive personality traits. So reach out first by spelling out the experience:

Rehearse

Have you ever tried practicing a speech to your own voice mail? You'll be surprised how similar the feeling is to an audience. By leaving a message to yourself, you can privately edit your intentions against your stage moment. Turn your cell into a microphone and rehearse anywhere. Practice makes perfect, it's true!

Emphasize

Communication is less than 7 percent verbal. This means you could recite every word correctly and only offer 7 pennies on the narrating dollar. What about tone, garland, and interplay? The sound and rhythm of a committed story-teller makes all the difference in the world. And literature agrees with grammar cues like *italics*, exclamations (!), and WORDS in all-caps. So let these intentions guide you and your voice. A bedtime story rarely intrigues without an interactive, emotional, component. So take the print to the next level!

Adapt

Actors truly experience the characters they play, and just let themselves go! This is important even to a narrator as a story is told. Consider the body language involvement of a pre-school teacher as they tell a story. Create an environment with your hands, and integrate learning opportunities. Christian Parables uses scriptures much like a kindergarten teacher uses lesson plans dedicated to arithmetic. The viewpoint should always be an interactive one.

Collaborate

Consider pausing in the middle of the story to ask your audience, "What do you think will happen next?" Give them the opportunity to react to the storyline and advise the characters. Also imagine making a play out of a parable. Invite family and friends for its cast of characters to rehearse for a short presentation. Include a narrator and another to explain the symbolism afterwards.

Host!

That's right! Be a biblical talk show host with you audience! As every Christian Parable blends scriptures with its scenes, your bible could create an instant-replay through its correlation. Lead a discussion on the (withheld) moral of the story. Later bring about the fun facts and the elaborations from the characters themselves (in Chapter 4). Doing this warms up the participation reflexes of an audience, making for a fun transition into a broader Bible study. Have fun with it! Well you seem ready! Good luck!

Chapter 2
Biblical Encore
Fun Facts, Fellowship, Scripture Index & more!

Each and every story offers what we like to call "a biblical encore." It provides it's very own lesson plan for an even more interactive Bible study.

With each New Parable you can:
- Offer symbolism and other hidden facts.
- Create an Instant Replay of its story scenes for traditional bible study.
- Use the scriptures as story clues before solving its mystery ending.
- Interact with the story characters through their Christian Challenges (in Chapter 4)

Also in this book:
- Presentation tips when sharing to an audience.
- A Scripture Index for quick reference

Wordplay Christian Parables 2 goes even further! As already demonstrated in the Introduction, each Christian Parable will include the following:

Fun Facts
Because these mystery-laced parables are animated by scripture, there are incredible confirmations and gospel combinations to enjoy! Have fun sharing these hidden clues with your listeners which cause The Thirsty Cup to "runneth over!"

Discussion Questions

The word "quest" is right in "question!" After sharing a Christian Parable, ask the ones each one will offer after the end. Go past the charm school qualities of a silent student. This is fellowship!

If you remember The Parable of the Hidden Smile in the first Christian Parables book, a hide-and-go-seek champion was thrilled to be found! In all fairness, he wasn't found as much as he was rescued by…an innocent question!

Character Interaction

Once again, some of the characters have their own challenges for you, off the pages!

Scripture Index

Be advised that the *Scripture Index* featured before the *Family Skit Versions* are listed in each parable's "story order," rather than in alphabetical order like the original *WordPlay Christian Parables* Book 1. However the additional *Index* featured in the last chapter is still listed alphabetically as before.

*Experience *Instant Replay Bible Study*, seeing how each scripture animates this new story below! Follow along with your own Bible or with our *Scripture Index*. Have Fun!

To reach the top of the water fountain, the thirsty schoolboys work together.

The Thirsty Cup Parable

"I'll lift you on the count-uh three," Frank tells Christian.

"One..." they say together, "Two... THREE!" Frank holds his friend Christian up, with all his child strength, and can hear the water now flowing.

"Hurry up Christian," Frank says as the seconds get heavier. "Is our cup almost full?"

"What cup?" Christian replies puzzled.

"The big cup we got from the cafeteria! We can save it for later. You're not even thirsty right now **(Psalms 143:5)**!"

"Yeah but this way, I will continue to feel full **(James 1:22)**."

"Forget using your mouth to feel full! Use your cup for a full fill **(Deuteronomy 11:18)** **(Proverbs 7:3)** **(Psalms 77:10:11)** **(Jonah 2:7)**!"

Christian's 'weight' becomes too much for Frank to hold, causing them both to fall **(Ecclesiastics 12:1)**.

"Sorry Frank!"

As Christian tries to return the favor, he simple isn't strong enough to lift his friend up.

The End

Story Symbolism
- Cafeteria = Wisdom
- Christian = Christians
- Fountain = Bible
- Lift = Support
- Water = Scriptures
- Cup = Heart
- Drink = Experience
- Thirsty = Troubled

Moral
Frank(ly) to every Christian, how can a "cup runneth over" if we drink directly from the faucet? Wisdom is feeling (and filling) The Word in your heart (both are needed) so you'll never urgently "thirst" for biblical instruction.

Character Interaction
The good news, for both Christian and Frank, is the sound of their much taller friend walking down that same hall. And that person is you! Can you them fill their cup? Can you store 20 scriptures? Take *Christian's Challenge!* Learn how on Chapter 4

A Maze In Grace (The Parable)

It's the amusement park's most popular attraction: *The Giant Maze*. And children run inside this life-sized mystery, knowing that only one child has ever completed it! Long ago the whole park watched Justin amaze a maze and become that child legend who found its path to victory. Remembering the only one who's ever won keeps *The Giant Maze* filled with kids vowing to be the second.

Still dizzy from her last rollercoaster ride is Little Gracie. She leans on the maze's Start sign, waiting to get her balance back. Plotting to win, Little Gracie stares inside *The Giant Maze's* scenery where everything appears black-and-white. But somehow its players look even dizzier than her! Children inside go from just wondering to just wandering. And some players, ashamed of their previous decisions, begin to trace the path of others to manipulate blame. Others just 'go wherever the wind blows' them, while some players stand still around its 'gray areas.' Little Gracie is now less dizzy and more concerned as players are losing more than the game. They're losing their energy, their since of direction, and their friendships. She can see clearly, from the Start, this maze is finishing players; not the other way around.

As the game goes on, players can only find the path to frustration. It's *everywhere* as some become aggressive, step on the backs of others, and hit the walls. Also unethical paths have some craftier players even pretend to be Justin, the only winner so far, so they can sell 'the winning directions' to others for their tokens. And only Grace sees them sneaking away past her and the *Start* area before their kid customers realize they've been cheated. And as players begin accusing others for being in their way and blocking their path, Grace drops her head in disappointment.

"It's just a *GAME!*" Grace yells to her school friends inside.

Grace throws her cotton candy to distract the emotions inside this life-size puzzle. But she misses her target and strikes the 'the man upstairs' operating the *Ferris Wheel*.

"Sorry!" Little Gracie apologizes.

"It's okay," the smiling Park Operator says while climbing down to return her treat. "I couldn't help but notice you starring into *The Giant Maze*. Do you think you'll go inside?"

"I was gonna," Little Gracie says, "but I probably won't. I'm not sure I can win this game. But I am sure this game isn't worth winning."

"Wow," the Park Operator reacts, "you sound just like Justin!"

Grace pauses, looking up at the Park Operator as he continues.

"Players don't enter in this maze, as much as this maze enters in its players! It is here where the lost *pretend* to be found, Grace. It is right *here* where artificial barriers, excuses, rules, and bad reasoning are made. I see too many kids follow everything *except* their heart until they can barely find themselves! Wisdom realizes it is, as you say, a game that's not worth winning."

"But Justin *did* win!"
"Uh huh… he sure did," smiles the Park Operator as Grace ponders to herself.
"*OOOH…* I've GOT it," Gracie says and runs quickly in a determined direction.

The park operator heads back upstairs and hears the whole park cheering. Already knowing why, he turns to see Grace running down the maze's *Finish* with every park light flashing. He smiles. With microphones in her face, Grace thanks 'the man upstairs' and begins to speak.

"The maze *itself* is the *REAL* barrier! We simply must go *around* it to find the path to victory! Any other way is a trap for our energy, our growth, and our potential."

The exhausted players lean in closer as Grace continues.

"And for those already inside, the correct way is the only direction this maze doesn't offer: up! So make contact with 'the man upstairs.' He has the Ferris (fairest) way to guide us' and take us from being lost in a maze, to being found in amazement… above and beyond this game."
The End

Story Symbolism
- Amusement Park = Earth
- Ferris (Fairest) Wheel = Heavenly Viewpoint
- Maze = Politics
- Barriers = Barriers
- Gray Areas = Controversy
- Players = Mankind
- Rollercoaster = Life's Ups and Downs
- Cotton Candy = Good Intentions
- Park Operator = God
- Little Gracie = Grace of God
- Justin = God's Glory
- Black and White Scenery = Alleged Easy Nature
- Fair Tokens = Money and Possessions

Moral
Life is a treasure hunt for smiles inside a pretty tricky maze. But with a little help for 'the man upstairs' you have "a maze in grace (*Amazing Grace*)." And the (narrow) path to victory awaits. Obstacles are rarely in the heart of the maze, but in the maze of the heart.

Share Your Thoughts
Is this parable your favorite?
Vote on our site!

Fun Facts

- Despite her dizziness and disappointment, Little Gracie was an "observer" the entire time (Proverbs 4:7) (Daniel 11:35) and literally from the very *Start*.
- Inspired by words of the Park Operator, Little Gracie literally "took those steps to win."
- Gracie's outcry that "it's *just* a *GAME*" wasn't enough to distract the "chaos inside." But her victory was.
- Child legend, Justin, is from the *Parable of The Hidden Smile* (in the first *Christian Parables* book) which animated a lesson in Salvation.

Discussion Questions

1. Do you think friendships in jeopardy gave Little Gracie extra motivation to win? Why or why not?
2. Initially "dizzy," Little Gracie waited as long as she needed "to get her balance back" from the (ups-and-downs) rollercoaster ride. How important was her decision?
3. Do you think *The Giant Maze's* black-and-white scenery (alleged easy nature) prevented its players from using their knowledge and wisdom?

The Parable of Ice-Cream Soup

"Wish me luck Mom," Faith says through her ice cream tasting. "When Dad arrives home, I'm gonna ask him for a bigger allowance."

"Good for you," Mom replies. "Do you think it might mean more chores for you to do?"

"I *hope* not," Faith replies, starring in her ice cream bowl. "I don't want *more* work! But I'm sure when Dad senses my excitement, and sees my '*please* face', it will be all I need to make this happen!"

"I see," Mom says smiling. "Well it's a good thing dishwashing is already a chore of yours! Are you ready?"

"Can I please finish my ice-cream first?"

"Well… why don't you put it in the oven for later?"

"But Mom… the oven is powered *ON* right now! My ice cream will turn to *soup*!"

Mom smiles at Faith and replies, "Always remember the lesson in this moment. Faith *without* works is like ice cream in an oven: only one power-switch away from having artificially warm feelings which surely melt the 'Rocky Road' *before* you finish."

The End

Story Symbolism

- Faith = Confidence
- Oven = Warm Feeling
- Dishes = Obedience
- Mom = Advisor
- Sunny = Believer
- Ice Cream = Desire
- Chores = Works
- Allowance = Blessing
- Dad = Heavenly Father

Moral

A desire cannot be held too long inside initially warm feelings (John 2:14). Like ice cream in an oven, faith without works just melts away until 'solid' action is taken.

Share Your Thoughts

Is this parable your favorite?
Vote on our site!

Fun Facts

- The "Rocky Road" symbolizes both a flavor and a common pathway to a substantial blessing.
- Faith could see the "power-switch" on the oven, but not in herself.
- The dynamic of "daddy's little girl" represents the already pleasing dynamic between (actual) Faith and God (Hebrews 11:6).
- The Mom's smiles represent a natural version of a "warm feeling," rather than artificial development.
- "Ice cream" has a homonym effect with "I scream:" an emotional destiny to unfulfilled desires.

Discussion Questions

1. How do you feel about the "wish me luck" statement Faith began with? What about her reply "I hope not!" Use scripture to support your reaction?

2. Share a time in your life when you may have metaphorically "stored your ice cream in an oven." What "extra work" could you have added?

3. Share a 'rocky road' with your own faith in your life.

The Parable of the Lawyer's Lullaby

The Lawyer invites the firm's Detective into his office.

"I need your help," the Lawyer says. "Could you investigate the courtroom in my last trial? Something weird was going on in there!"

"Sure," the Detective agrees, "what happened?"

"Well every time I tried to cross-examine a witness, they became very sleepy, almost instantly! Some even fell asleep on the stand. And the Judge just let them leave, one by one, cheating me out of getting their testimony."

"Wait-a-second," the Detective replies, "maybe *THAT* was the *motive*! Without your evidence, the case would have to be dismissed, right? Are you sure the witnesses were *really* asleep? Maybe they were just pretending to be for a creative escape."

"You know what," the Lawyer's agrees, "I was in the same courtroom and I was *never* sleepy!"

"And you said the Judge simply excused them from the witness stand. Maybe the Judge was in on this! How else could this sleeping plan work? *Forget* the courtroom conditions! We should investigate the Judge. What's his name?"

"It was… wow, I'm can't remember right now."

"No problem," the Detective assures. "What about the defendant's name? We can go from that?"

"The defendant's name is…. is in my briefcase. Let me find it for you."

The detective waits as the Lawyer scours his entire office.

"You know what," the Detective interrupts, "your case is so *unique* that I'm sure the courthouse can identify it and help me with the details. I'll head over there now."

"Thank you Detective. I know it's here somewhere. I'll call you with the information."

Arriving at the scene of this sleeping phenomenon, the Detective has the extra challenge of investigating without any names, case numbers, timeframes, or even a specific courtroom! But before he can experience his full dilemma, the Detective sees the Lawyer's briefcase in a room which seems empty, until he hears the sound of someone snoring. It is a female Juror fast asleep in the jury panel.

Stunned at her true sleep mode, the Detective knows there is more to discover. So he awakes the Juror.

"We should move you out this room, Miss. I wanna investigate what's causing everyone here to fall asleep."

"Save your investigation," the Juror responds, "it was the Lawyer."

"The Lawyer?"

"It was the Lawyer's lullaby of a case," The Juror replies through a yawn. "Witness after witness took the stand. And no matter honest, informative, or helpful their testimony was… the lawyer kept asking the same questions over and over again, like they *never* answered! And the more exhausted the witness got, the more excited the lawyer became until the Judge declared a mistrial. It was weird, pointless, and lot of other things! But the one thing it *wasn't* was coffee."

"I realize the trial is over," the Detective says, "but I'm gonna cross-examine *YOU* now! The Lawyer complained about witnesses falling sleeping *before* he got the chance to question, and not *after* like you describe. Can you explain that?"

"That's not true. But I can still explain this because, when I'm not a Juror, I'm a doctor. And based on the Lawyer's behavior, it's clear he has amnesia."

The Detective's eyes widen as she continues.

"I don't think the Lawyer even *remembers* how repetitive and ineffective he was being, or how rude he was to the Judge. In fact, I'd be surprised he even remembered the Judge's name!"

The Detective's eyes widen more.

"I bet all this Lawyer remembers are the mysterious conditions where he didn't get his way… and felt dismissed."

The End

Story Symbolism

- Lawyer (Prosecutor) = Reasoning
- Detective = Knowledge
- The Firm = Heart
- Courtroom = Conversation
- Witnesses = Clarity
- Sleepiness = Weariness (Spiritual Exhaustion)
- Briefcase = Bible
- Juror = Truth
- Case = Argument
- Judge = God Almighty
- Lawyer's Condition = Dismissive Behavior

Moral

Strife changes the Truth for itself. Peace changes itself for the Truth. Any "condition" that exhausts the process of knowledge itself can only be the beginning of a "cycle" of unproductive embarrassment and even more mystery. Don't be "a lawyer with amnesia." If we don't change our absence of mind, then we don't mind our absence of change.

Share Your Thoughts

Is this parable your favorite?
Vote on our site!

Fun Facts

- This entire court story never mentioned a defendant, but only "something weird going on."
- Both the Lawyer and the Detective shared the same firm(ness), with initial reflexes toward each other (Proverbs 21:2).
- The Detective's discovery, without any real details, symbolizes the promise: seek and you shall find (Jeremiah 29:13).
- The case was officially declared a mistrial (temporary); it was not dismissed (final) (Matthew 3:2).

Discussion Questions

1. How would you rate the interrogation level of the Detective toward other characters?
2. What other reasons are possible for why the Detective was willing to begin an investigation with "an extra challenge" of no real details? Share a similar story where someone's determination skipped the details like the Detective.
3. How different would the story have been if the Detective were never called in?

Character Interaction

What kind of skills would a detective need to have to investigate without any details, like this one? Read the Detective's *Charity versus Ability* essay and "discover" 3 essential things to be effective in any "case (Chapter 4)!"

Peculiar Treasure (The Parable) (Poetry)

No man exists with my enchanted wish
to craft a love affair with God and trust His management,
and graph above the stares I've gotten from abandonment
But yet, I couldn't understand it when HE granted this!

Imagine this: God said, "Enough repairs! You must be fair.
Prepare MY coming from upstairs
to interrupt these prayers.
From your heart, the truth is clever
But putting these clues together….
gives you your measure of 'peculiar treasure.'
I have merged your truth with pleasure many years ago.
I have blurred you views in pressure.
Any tear would know!
You empty fears should show exactly how,
so don't attack ME now…"
Then HE appeared in those attracting clouds.

With all my prayers that last for paragraphs,
I didn't dare to ask a thing except to spare the laugh
and share the facts
I said, "I'm ready for the clues you'll part with."
God replied, "How shall I start this
to prove your heart rich?
I have evidence, Heaven sent, of your enchanted wish.
It has a puzzle-tested smile
that's left your struggle less than mild.

The first to dance with
in your circumstances,
It's like a Couple blessed with child,
within one huddle-essence style!
Still guessing? It was my blessing to your urgent request.
And Mother Nature's still requesting a paternity test.
'Cause who'd believe the Earth could surface this?
Somehow your birth certificate goes perfect with this wish.

But only hear It when you listen in,
for a rest above words.
The Holy Spirit is my synonym
for 'Heaven on Earth.'
So when I bless a fellow Christian
to digest My Melo System …
It proves your measure of peculiar treasure…. forever."
The End

*In no way is this parables use of "peculiar treasure"
intended to compete with or replace the original reference
to Israelites in Exodus. It is merely symbolic of an equal
since of appreciation in the "new" temple of the New
Testament.

Poetry Symbolism
- Man = Christians
- Enchanted Wish = Oneness with God
- Peculiar Treasure = The Holy Spirit
- Upstairs = Heaven

Moral

No one can afford to overlook our current spiritual shepherd: The Holy Spirit. Ever since Jesus rose again, our Leader is so close to us... that It's inside us! And It's influence is so overwhelming that even the world acknowledges it through other nicknames (like Conscience). So during our spiritual journey to the New Testament's "Promised Land (Heaven)," in this wilderness of a world, look no further for a sign. Look inside! God Bless.

Share Your Thoughts

Is this parable your favorite?
Vote on our site!

Fun Facts

- The man was unknowingly interacting with and through his "enchanted wish" the entire time (John 15:26)!
- Notice that God respected the man's request to "spare the laugh and share the facts."
- The "prayers that last for paragraphs" represent long, lengthy, traditional religious formats.
- Notice the easy-going, one-on-one dynamic the entire time.
- Realize that God actually did come down specifically to talk with the man about a better relationship.

Discussion Questions

1. When God jokingly said "don't attack ME now," what could HE have been making a subtle reference to?
2. Elaborate on the lyrics "...from your heart, the truth is clever."
3. What do you suppose God meant by saying, "Enough repairs?"
4. God respected the man's request to "spare the laugh and share the facts." How unique might this approach be compared to others with God?

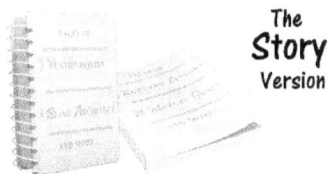

The
Story
Version

Batteries Not Included (The Parable)

"Here you go," Corey says dropping his coins into Jeff's hands.

"Sold," Jeff says, "I have more baseball cards for the same price."

"Wow," Corey replies, "even after all the one's you sold at school today, you *still* have some left? What are you saving up for anyway?"

"Come on, the cards are in my room."

"Wow," Corey says walking inside, "you sure have a lot of new batteries lying around in here! You should look for a way to sell *these* instead to afford whatever you... what are you saving up for?"

Tommy ponders how to answer until Chris realizes on his own.

"Wait-a-minute," Chris says, "you sell your baseball cards... to buy all these batteries?"

"Yeah," Jeffrey admits. "It's the only way to keep playing my video game! All these batteries are for this game player."

"Lemme see," Corey picks up this demanding device. "Wait a second! This game player has a chord attached! Just plug it in, silly!"

"Corey, it's too uncomfortable when it's plugged in! Who likes being tethered to the wall? I wanna feel further away and able to move around more!"

"So… you're actually *hoping* to 'sell out' your birthday gift of baseball cards, just to afford your plan to feel *LESS* connected?" Sounds to me like a 'different game' with an 'extra controller.'"

Jeff considers this as Corey continues.

"How far away and detached do you need to be inside the comfort of your own home? You're right beside an uninterrupted power source, which your Father already paid for! Keep the rest of your cards, keep the quality of your time and play. Stay connected."
The End

Story Symbolism
- Home = God's Presence
- Baseball Cards = Gifts & Purpose
- Birthday Gift = Unique Gifts from God
- Sell = Trade (Sacrifice)
- Game Player = Heart
- Video Game = Lifestyle
- Power Source = God
- Batteries = Spiritual Distance
- Chord = Relationship with God

Moral
Direct fellowship with God will perfect the needs of a man's heart. But preferring more (cordless) distance begins a cycle of control and sacrifice of your God-given gifts until you have completely "sold out." Don't be your own Delilah and "cut yourself short." It's too costly for anyone. *"Start over!"*

Share Your Thoughts
Is this parable your favorite?
Vote on our site!

Fun Facts
- The baseball cards symbolize the potential to discover extreme value.
- Jeff's character was inspired by Esau
- Jeff's full first name (Jeffrey) initially sounds "free."
- The moment where Jeff "ponders how to answer" symbolizes rehearsed public opinion.
- Corey's discovery of the chord did not surprise Tommy. He already realized it!

Discussion Questions
1. Despite realizing the chord before Chris, Tommy prefaced his dilemma by insisting the batteries were "the only way to get playing time!" What might his motivation had been?

Character Interaction
Take the *Stay Connected Challenge*
Continue to Chapter 4

The
Story
Version

The Parable of the Waitress's Tip

"Well hello again Eugene," the Waitress approaches. "What will it be today? Your usual lunch special?"

"Well that kinda depends," Eugene replies. "Is it true that you guys are closing early today?

"Yeah," the Waitress confirms, "we'll be closing early right before dinner time."

"I see," Eugene says handing the menu back, "I'll have Combo One… Two… Three-Four-Five and Combo Six…with a Diet Cola please."

"Well if your co-workers are all dining here, you could use our banquet room with a bigger table!"

"No… this is all gonna be for me, just me," Eugene says sadly. "See I've been struggling with something inside me that just never feels full! My appetite mysteriously just keeps on ticking to extra weight, but won't wait extra! So I'll need to eat Dinner for Lunch today too! I apologize, I shouldn't bother you with my problems."

"That's okay," the Waitress says. "Let me bring you an appetizer immediately. I'll be right back!"

Almost before he can agree, the Waitress returns to his table with the appetizer as promised.

"Thank you, really."

Time goes by without the Waitress in sight. Finally Eugene sees her and gestures urgently.

"Thanks so much for this appetizer so far. But whatever you guys haven't cooked yet, please don't! I can't explain why, but I feel *great* inside with no hunger after that miniature-sized appetizer! And of course I'll gladly pay for..."

"We didn't make any of them," the Waitress smiles. "I knew we wouldn't need too."

"Really," Eugene says surprised, "how?"

"Well... I only work here to put myself through college to become a Nutritionist. So I am educated on the natural way digestion works! The platter I gave you is organic: free from the artificial preservatives designed to keep people hungry."

"Are you serious? There are ingredients like that?"

"Oh yeah," the waitress sits down with Eugene and whispers, "there are chemicals to make bread rise more attractively, artificial sweeteners to change energy levels. And unfortunately Eugene, I'm dishing about the dishes *here*! I just found out today that this place uses them."

"So *this* is the reason for my appetite."

"It's also the reason for this place closing early. The Chef quit... right after I did this morning! In fact, I'm not even supposed to be here right now! But I've been hiding around so I can warn my favorite customers."

"I can't thank you enough," Eugene reacts. "Can I pay you for the appetizer?"

"It's on me," the Waitress says, "Eugene you're a great and generous customer. So *THIS* time let *me* give *YOU* a tip: since this is the only restaurant in town, start growing your own healthy foods, and learn how to cook.

The appetite you once had is *nothing* compared to the appetite of this business. It's like a "bottomless pit!"
The End

Story Symbolism
- Restaurant = Earth
- Appetite = Purpose
- Hunger = Void in the Heart
- Organic = Natural Intent
- Waitress = Truth
- Eugene = Mankind
- Chef = Compromise
- Artificial Ingredients = Man-made Influence
- Cooking = Bible Study
- Bread Chemical = Leaven of the Pharisees
- Menu = Earthly Satisfaction
- Artificial Sweeteners = Vain Motivation
- Appetizer = Bread of Life & Fruits of Holy Spirit

Moral
There's no appetite to sin around the spiritual "bread" of life, "fruits" of the Holy Spirit, and a "cup" that runneth over! Avoid the "aftertaste" of vanity. And always remember that nothing "serves" a man better than the truth. God bless!

Share Your Thoughts
Is this parable your favorite?
Vote on our site!

Fun Facts

- Realize the quitting order: first the Waitress (Truth), then the Chef (Compromise).
- Eugene's order, without looking at the menu, symbolizes that he's "seen it all before."
- The news about the restaurant's early closing probably came from "a sign."
- Notice the Waitress reflex to "sit down and whisper with" Eugene, when he pursued more knowledge.

Discussion Questions

1. Overall how would you rate the Waitress's customer service skills?
2. Why do you think the Waitress responded to Eugene's needs first, before offering the bigger picture?
3. How do you feel about the Waitress hiding around after quitting to warn her favorite customers?
4. Notice how "that's okay" was the Waitress's reply, when Eugene felt he shared too much of his personal challenges to her. How beneficial was this?

Character Interaction

She's ready to 'dish about those dishes!' After all, the Waitress no longer works for them anymore, right? As the Waitress continues hiding around to warn more customers, you have a unique opportunity to help her spread this fulfilling message further! Read and share her rhyming mission as a *Camouflaged Prophet* in Chapter 4. God bless!

The Parable of the Counselor's Gift

"It's a gift," the School Counselor explains to the news reporter. And it seems to be her answer to every question, even though *she* asked for this interview. "It's a gift" is all she offers to explain her sudden popularity. Surveys score this School Counselor at number one: more admired than the Principal, the Coach, and all the teachers combined! The news reporter continues trying for a variety of answers.

"Well what about the scoring pattern, Counselor? I notice you score highest with kids involved in school fights. Could you talk *specifically* about how you inspire them? How do you do it?

The School Counselor does open up more. But her responses seem very basic with nothing unique enough to justify her isolated success. From "let you smile be your umbrella" to "forget your troubles and just get happy," the journalist sits both confused and unimpressed. His next question probes deeper.

"And despite 'the gift' you have, school fights have *actually* been on the rise! Now it's actually been suggested that some kids are literally fighting to see you. Some believe their misbehavior is only done to skip the long waiting line to make an appointment with you, Counselor!

How do you respond? Or maybe you have a different theory to helps us understand."

"Well I think that *maybe* it's a challenge for me to be even *less* selfish with my gift."

"I see," replies the now frustrated news reporter. "Well... would it be okay, Counselor, to see you in action one day?"

"I'll share my gift, *sure!*"

The next day another school fight occurs. The one-sided battle between an Honor student and his bully increases the crowd and the chaos longer than usual. So the Counselor is desperately called. Live news cameras follow behind them as they walk into the Principals Office.

"Okay," the Counselor says entering inside "where are the boys?"

"We separated them," the secretary answers. "Bully is Room 1, honor student Room 2."

"Thanks." The Counselor turns toward the Reporter. "Okay I *always* deal with the more likely victim first which is the honor student in Room 2. I'll speak to him alone."

"Absolutely!" The news reporter says cuing the cameraman.

As the Counselor heads inside, her school fans eavesdrop next to the door for the magical conversation they expect. But the words they can make out are the same phrases *they* use: "let your smile be your umbrella," and "forget your troubles and just get happy!" Five minutes pass, the door re-opens, and an instantly overjoyed schoolboy walks out.

"Amazing," a fan says. "It truly is a gift!"

The little boy is now even trying to make arraignments to talk with the other boy.

"That's so mature of you young man," another fan says, "but I think the Counselor is first!"

"Actually," The Counselor says, "the security guards are first! It's our school policy to always send them in first to determine if the bigger aggressor is calm enough and I'm safe enough to go in."

"Sure!" the news reporter continues to observe.

Security guards go in and quickly return shaking their heads against it. The Counselor as she head nods back.

"Well it looks like I'm done here," the Counselor says. "We'll all just need to be more patient with the other boy."

"Sure!" The first boy agrees giving her a hug.

"Incredible," the cameraman admits to the reporter.

"Thank you for coming." The counselor says to the news reporter. Pulling him closer, the Counselor whispers in his ear, "I told you… it's a gift."

Applause surrounds the Principals office as she leaves smiling.

Still curious about the increase in school fights, the reporter asks to interview the other boy. Immediately the guards fiercely block the door. But even quicker are other school officials insisting the entire news team leave. And suddenly the mystery becomes clear to him.

"Oh my…" the reporter runs in the other direction past everyone with his confused cameraman. "I think we have an even *bigger* story."

Rushing to the secretary, the reporter stares in disbelief.

"You *switched* the boys and the rooms!"

The secretary shivers as the crowd develops.

"You *tricked* the Counselor into consoling the *bully*, and ignoring the real victim! And you used the security guards to block off the right entrance!"

The security guards rush to the exit with their guilt, pushing news cameras away.

"So the *REAL* reason fights keep happening here is because the School Counselor bullies the *guilt* these bullies have developed from their own bullying until it disappears!"

The crowd stares with the cameras as he continues.

"It's *NOT* a gift! It's a deception that you're causing the Counselor and everyone else to believe! Oh, you are in big trouble. Someone get me to The Principal!"

"Good luck with that," replies the secretary, "you won't believe this *either* but I was *just* doing my job! And I don't work for HIM. I work for *her*."

The End

Story Symbolism

- School Counselor = Simplicity
- Secretary (Assistant): Manipulation
- News Reporter = Righteousness (Hunger and Thirst)
- School Fights = Strife
- Cameraman = Public Viewpoint
- Survey = Opinions
- The Principal = The Principle of Righteousness
- Teacher - Official Advisors
- School = The World
- Interview - Testing the Spirits
- Gift = Presents (of Presence)
- Honor Student = Wisdom
- Bully = Folly
- Security Guards = Advice
- School Policy = Tradition

Moral

Simplicity is willing to manipulate itself and betray wisdom *just* to be popular (believe it or not). So its mysterious 'gift' that merely sounds like presents (presence) should be fairly questioned (or interviewed). Simplicity is a lukewarm intervention more likely to protect vanity, and block truth. Any authority lacking a real "hunger and thirst for righteousness" will only increase the ongoing struggle between wisdom and folly.

Share Your Thoughts

Is this parable your favorite?
Vote on our site!

Fun Facts

- It was the Counselor who asked for the interview, not the other way around (Proverbs 16:19).
- The Counselor's private whisper animates a reprobate mind (Romans 1:28).
- The (non-questionable) school policy (tradition) was the only thing the Counselor was specific about.
- The eavesdropping fans could not make out any questions (just rhetorical statements).

Discussion Questions

1. Interpret the very last line in the story: "I don't work for HIM, I work for her."
2. What do you think the other boy would have told the news reporter (in scripture)?
3. Imagine how the Counselor's fans felt around the news crew? Explain why.

Character Interaction

No one got a chance to hear from the other boy: the real Honor Student. But you can! Read his essay: *The Top 20 Biblical Signs of a Fool* in Chapter 4.

The
Story
Version

The Parable of the Calendar's Watch

The cheers get louder and louder as the Celebrity walks inside the store. She shakes the business promoter's hand and then waves hers to the cheering crowd: each one with a calendar in their hand. Simply buying this store's calendar today earns an autograph and chance to meet the star in person! And with her fan club of jumping girls and blushing boys, this store has already sold out. So the promoter rushes out to make more copies. Meanwhile the cheers follow the Celebrity as she meets, poses for pictures, and finally signs everyone's calendar. But in the corner of her eye, she sees a separate stand with a gentleman selling another product. *Whatever* it is doesn't appear to be doing nearly as well as the calendars.

"Mark your calendars folks," the promoter announces, "because she, and our wonderful calendars, will be returning back here soon!"

Applause erupts again as the event planners thank her. And as the chasing crowd moves to the left, she gets a much clearer view of the gentleman salesman. Still trying to make out exactly what product he's selling, she leaves for lunch.

Inside the restaurant with her agent, the Celebrity notices people in her VIP section disappear, running toward a new arriving guest. She realizes it's the same less popular gentleman vendor at the marketplace event. The older gentleman hands out the same mysterious product to all who simply ask. And to the Celebrity's surprise, she realizes that even her agent has left their table to shake the gentleman's hand.

"Just who is this guy?" the Celebrity wonders, "and what is he selling?" The gentleman smiles at her stare and whispers an equally mysterious request in her agent's ear. And filled with excitement, her agent takes his hand and walks the gentleman to the Celebrity's table.

"I'm a huge fan of you." The gentleman says to the Celebrity.

"I really appreciate it," the Celebrity replies looking around for his calendar copy to autograph. "Thank you sir!"

"I was just talking with your agent, hoping you would consider endorsing *my* product instead of Mr. Calendar's."

"Oh … we *ACCEPT!*" The agent says impulsively.

"Well *wait*-a-second," the Celebrity laughs along with the gentleman. "I would like to know more if I may!"

"Of course!" The gentleman says sincerely.

"Please have a seat, sir!"

"Here take *my* chair, Sir!" The agent offers. "You guys discuss the details while I'll find our waiter for another chair!"

As the gentleman sits down next to her, customers peek with smiles and thumbs up, cheering on the lucky one. It is unclear to the Celebrity which one she is. The gentleman begins.

"I know what Mr. Calendar has agreed to pay you. But I am prepared to offer you even more!"

"Well with all due respect, sir. Your product didn't seem as popular at the store event."

"You can't always believe what you see," the gentleman says smiling. "I own the entire marketplace. Mr. Calendar rented today's limited time here. I was just keeping an eye on my store."

The Celebrity leans in more as he continues.

"Today's shoppers only see the decorations of a crafty businessman: celebrity appeal, commercials, and a chance to party with the majority for a price. But the big picture has Mr. Calendar in huge debt. He secretly needs your endorsement for access to your fans, which means a chance to sell items and be less 'in the red.'

"Well how can Mr. Calendar afford me then?"

"He can't! Mr. Calendar put tricks in your contract to avoid paying you."

The Celebrity's begins to remember her contract's complicated language.

"But his business tactics go even further!" The gentleman points to the Celebrity's sample calendar. "Look closer at his calendar that everyone bought today. Do you see anything odd about it?"

"Oh my goodness!" the Celebrity says while pointing, "It's *LAST* year's calendar!"

"That's right. Mr. Calendar is all about the money even when it means deliberately selling items that are worthless and outdated with no real value. He uses your fans' appetite to meet you as camouflage."

The Celebrity's eyes open almost a wide as her fans after seeing her.

"We've got to do something, Sir! Some people are living according to that outdated material."

"For all his offenses, I will to drive him out soon. But right now I am more concerned about the unsuspecting customers."

"Well if it's *your* business, what are you waiting for, sir? You could do it right now."

"For the customers' sake, the real competition is between his craftiness and my truth. And this is exactly the message I would like you to share while endorsing my *free* product. Mr. Calendar won't be able to compete."

"Why… is your product a calendar too?"

"My product is *SO* much better than a calendar."

"So let me get this straight," the Celebrity clarifies. "You want to hire me for a celebrity endorsement of your *free* product: a product that you believe will somehow put Mr. Calendar out of business because, in your opinion, your product satisfies *BETTER* than a calendar! What is this product you created?"

"It's called eternal life."

The End

Moral

Sin is about as cheap and outdated as a Clearance Sale on last year's calendar. Buy Eternal Life, freely given by God's grace. The children of God are like anointed celebrities appealing to the heart of man. The real celebration is salvation. Start spreading the news!

Share Your Thoughts

Is this parable your favorite?
Vote on our site!

Story Symbolism
- The Celebrity = *You!*
- The Gentleman = God
- Agent = Heart
- Crowd = Mankind
- Fans = Family and Friends (of You)
- Event = Life
- Calendar = Sin (For a Season)
- Store = Earth
- Restaurant = Spiritual Realm
- Endorse = Live For
- Autograph = Proclaim
- Mr. Calendar = Satan
- Payment = Blessing
- Contract = Supernatural Intentions
- Restaurant Staff = Angels
- Rented Time = Earthy Time for a Season

Fun Facts
- No one ate at the table while the gentleman spoke, unless you count "HIS every word (Matthew 4:4)."
- The Celebrity first view of the gentleman at the store was from the "right" angle.
- The agent (heart) demonstrated the same fan club setting for the Gentlemen (God).
- The excitement of the agent (heart) caused behavior out of traditional character, as it should.
- The whisper into the agent's ear represents the privacy between God's voice and his children.
- The gentleman's "smile at her stares" represents the God's reaction to anyone seeking his face.

- Notice the gentleman never actually had a calendar himself (pure, without sin).
- The gentleman referred to their setting as "my" restaurant, in addition to the marketplace he owns.
- The owner was against a full monopoly.
- The gentleman being patient with his intervention was ultimately to protect the naïve customers from the effect of a riot.
- The gentleman adjusted himself to the Celebrity's auditioning norms before showing her the big picture.
- Not one episode of envy centered around the restaurant.
- The customers at the restaurant symbolize "new creatures" being served (still competing to serve God).
- The gentleman beginning statement, "I'm a huge fan of you," animates how God loved us first.
- The gentleman did not speak competitively; he only spoke truthfully.

Discussion Questions

1. When has your own "agent (heart)" been moved toward the gentleman (God) almost independently out of natural excitement, like in the story? Share this moment.
2. If The Gentleman claimed his success was self-made by his "blood, sweat, and tears," which scripture(s) supports this.
3. How do you feel about the gentleman's stating "the real competition is between his craftiness and my truth?"

Character Interaction

The story never mentioned what The Celebrity is famous *for*! She is a musical communicator (Rapper). But now, with her new endorsement deal, she is a new and improved Christian Rapper. Experience her uplifting lyrics in *Perception Bearer* in Chapter 4. Have fun!

Couples Therapy Parable (Poetry)

Past his years of mixing wrath with tears
and wedding rings,
none of his tactics cleared the atmosphere.
And everything that's happened here is obvious
I follow this, as their psychologist,
reluctant to acknowledge this scene:
A narcissistic groom, it seems,
their heart logistics doomed if we
can't quickly earn some apologies
As their exes cheer against them,
and their kid's the clearest victim,
let us learn from analogies.

Story Symbolism

- Couple = God & Mankind
- Kid = Jesus
- Narcissism = Pride
- Exes = Lucifer, Fallen Angels
- Psychologist = The Holy Spirit
- Apologies = Repentance
- Wedding Rings = Covenants
- Tactics = Non-direct Strategy

Moral

There's always a *U* and *I* in "communication." But the distance varies by perception! Therefore, it is so important to find a common denominator (like parables) when relaying to one another, both in and out The Kingdom.

Share Your Thoughts

Is this parable your favorite?
Vote on our site!

Fun Facts

- The pride is followed by the words "it seems," suggesting that maybe unawareness is the root of the problem.
- The "narcissistic groom (it seems)" character is interchangeable between God and Man since they share the same image (Genesis 1:26) (but of course this describes Man).
- Although the urgency was to "earn some apologies," the ultimate goal was to rebuild the relationship.

Discussion Questions

1. How do you interpret the phrase "mixing wrath with tears?"
2. What might the fact that "none of his tactics cleared the atmosphere" reveal about the groom (mankind)?

The
Story
Version

The Parable of the Blindfold

Thomas tilts with his telephone in the early morning, preparing to leave a message.

"Yes *hello*… I'm a patient at *The Lucky Ones Clinic*. And I need to cancel my appointment today with my doctor, Lady Luck. Something came up. But I have enough of your *4-Leaf-Clover* cream to last me until we can reschedule. Thanks! Bye."

Thomas drops the phone next to a map he is still starring at, along with a business card he kept, matching the addresses. And practically tip-toeing to his car, Thomas proceeds out of town to the new destination.

"Hi," a hospital clerk greets Thomas as he arrives inside, "can I help you sir?"

"Yes good morning! I'm Thomas Walker and have an appointment with Doctor Powers."

"Sure! Please follow me to the office."

Thomas continues to look around ensuring he's not noticed by anyone from his town.

"Good morning," the new doctor walks inside, "is it Thomas Walker?"

"Doctor Powers," Thomas says shaking her hand. "Thanks for agreeing see me."

"My pleasure. But we're on a first name basis here. Please just call me Faith."

"You got it! Faith, I heard about you through my friend Christian. She tells me you're the best!"

"Well it's *actually* a team effort," Faith smiles. "Let's make it your turn to feel better! How can I help?"

"Well my skin type is extremely sensitive to sunlight. And I live in a desert, with no real way to block it! Until I can afford to move, I've been using a medicated *4-Leaf-Clover* cream to lessen the effects."

"Wow," Faith says, "someone must have to really 'lay it on thick!'"

"Yeah, my original doctor does. It helps a little, but it's really expensive! And she insists it's the only way! So I guess I'm here for a second opinion."

"Sure," Faith replies, "let's run some tests and I think I can help you with that."

Much to the surprise of Thomas, Faith actually begins by checking his blood pressure.

"Oh this is good news!" Faith says, "Thomas I'm happy to offer you a cheaper and better alternative. Based on these tests, your condition actually needs *physical* therapy, not medicated creams. And, if you like, we can begin right now!"

"Absolutely!"

"So let's head to my operating room. And, for this to work, I'll need to blindfold you first. Then I'll take your hand and lead you inside a machine where you'll vary your speeds when I tell you to. Are you ready?"

Although unsure how this will help, Thomas submits. Faith begins her unique procedure.

Time passes by unnoticed as Thomas awakes from a deep sleep. And he finds himself somehow back inside his bed at home! But before he can call this whole experience a dream, Thomas notices a doctor's note signed by Faith. But as he holds it up to the window to read it, no sunlight shines through. In fact there's no heat to be felt either! Puzzled, Thomas turns on a lamp. And he immediately notices his incredibly smooth, cooled, healthy skin.

"Oh my!" Thomas drops the letter and runs to his mirror. He looks completely revitalized and renewed. But along with his image reflection, he sees a new, giant object outside his window. Turning around, Thomas finally realizes what has happened: somehow a mountain has moved to block the sunlight from the house, forever protecting his skin condition.

After hours of pinching himself and crying tears of joy, Thomas returns to Faith's note:

'Keep the rest of these mustard seeds, Thomas. Doctor's orders!'
To Be Continued

*Stand firm with Faith as this parable continues and Faith is tested!

Story Symbolism

- Lady Luck = Superstitions, Myths
- Dr. Faith Powers = Faith
- (Doubting) Thomas = Mankind
- Business Card = Change
- Map = Mind State
- Prescriptions = Insistence
- Desert = Deserted Place
- Christian = Fellowship
- Skin = Potential
- Sunlight = Exposure to Doubt
- Physical Therapy = Action

Moral, Discussion Questions, & Fun Facts revealed after full story*

The Blindfold Parable 2: Testing Faith

Thomas holds up the remaining mustard seeds, literally cool enough to wonder if he'll ever need the *4 Leaf Clover* cream again. Perhaps Faith knew was she was doing after all, though Thomas couldn't determine how. As he keeps pondering how, his phone rings.

"Hello?" Thomas answers.

"Good afternoon! I'm Katelyn with the *Good News Team*, preparing you in advance that we'll be doing a story on the miracle in your town. Did you by chance witness any of while it was happening? Could we interview you?"

"I did not witness it. But I think I know how it happened! Please come over."

Moments later the doorbell rings.

"Coming," Thomas yells while adjusting his best tie.

He tried calling Faith, but couldn't reach her. He retrieves the business card that started it all. And as he arrives, he opens his door to another memory.

"Oh...Lady Luck." Thomas reacts, "I didn't know you made house calls! I appreciate it but right now's not a good t..."

"She's not a *real* doctor, Thomas! Faith is a fraud."

"How did you know that..."

"I *saw* you go in her office, okay." Lady Luck explains while massaging her rabbit's foot. "Luckily, I was 'at the right place at the right time,' Thomas. I came to take you back to *The Lucky Ones Clinic* and hopefully undo whatever Faith did."

"Are you kidding?" Thomas replies, "With all due respect, the way Faith works is more effective. Before I even *knew* this mountain was moved, I rested better. I didn't just sit still and let everyone 'rub it in,' I finally got up! I *walked* with Faith."

"And when you walked with Faith…. I bet you were blindfolded."

"I was," Thomas replies in curiosity. "Why?"

"Well," Lady Luck laughs, "let me show you what you didn't see as you walked blindly with Faith in another room, increasing your speed."

Lady Luck hands Thomas a picture of him blindfolded at Faith's office, on a treadmill.

"How can this be real?" Thomas says through embarrassment.

"I *told* you she's a con-artist! Why is this so… oh I see! You thought Faith moved this mountain?"

Laughter increases in Lady Luck, as Thomas sees the *Good News Team* arriving for an interview.

"Hey," Lady Luck grabs Thomas arm, "this town's not big enough for *two* doctors. So if you even mention Faith to them, I'll embarrass you with these pictures and your gullible story."

Thomas runs emotionally past everyone and into his car, to everyone's surprise. Driving off quickly, he can still feel the laugher from Lady Luck and all who she might tell.

Once again, Thomas retrieves the business card and drives even more intently than before.

Walking past the secretary, and into Faith's procedure room, Thomas looks around and the true account of a treadmill.

"Thomas," Faith walks in, "is everything okay?"
"How could you play with my feelings like this?"
"What are you talking about?"
"I *trusted* you!"
"Yeah… and you're condition has improved, Thomas! You are making a… *molehill* out of a mountain!"
"So… it's true?" Thomas clarifies. "*You* moved that mountain? How? And why did you need me to embarrass myself by moving around on a treadmill?"
"Thomas let me show you." Faith says pulling out the familiar blindfold. "Perception contaminates the procedure! The challenge is not me shielding this place from you; it is me shielding you from *THIS* place. You don't need thick-skin when you're not exposed."

Thomas continues to listen.

"As for the physical therapy? Well… we had to get your heart pumping, at least long enough to move past your 'doubting, Thomas!' And we had to work together. Remember when I told you this is a team effort? We needed each other's energy. And apparently it was enough for you to work with!"
"What do you mean by 'enough for me to work with?"

"Oh ye of little faith," The doctor smiles, "I didn't move that mountain. *You* did!"

The End

Moral

Faith is a biblically-approved, blindfolded journey within the spiritual rights we have as God's children. And the celebration belongs to the "team effort" between the grace of God and the willingness of Christians to walk with it. Faith is a process too amazing to be confused with luck.

Share Your Thoughts

Is this parable your favorite?
Vote on our site!

Story Symbolism

- Lady Luck = Superstitions, Myths
- The Clinic = Challenges
- Dr. Faith Powers = Faith
- (Doubting) Thomas = Mankind
- Business Card = Change
- Map = Mind State
- Prescriptions = Insistence
- Desert = Deserted Place
- Christian = Fellowship
- Skin = Potential
- Sunlight = Exposure to Doubt
- Physical Therapy = Action
- Treadmill = Obstacles
- *Good News Team* = Joyful Testimony

Fun Facts

- The words "doubting" and "Thomas" appear together toward the story's end, mentioning the disciple "Doubting Thomas."
- The mustard seeds left by Dr. Faith attribute the biblical process (Matthew 17:20)
- The doctor's full name (Faith Powers) is designed like an incomplete sentence. It is "a team effort" with mankind.
- Lady Luck had her "practice" as a doctor in the desert (deserted place) where Thomas lived.
- As Thomas explained his predicament to Faith, his statement that he couldn't afford to "move" is a double meaning.
- When Faith said that "someone" was "really laying it on thick," she never said who!

Discussion Questions

1. How did you (or your listeners) feel when the picture of the treadmill was revealed? Share a story of your own when your faith was tested.
2. Why do you suppose Lady Luck followed her doubts in Faith with a threat to embarrass Thomas if he mentioned her to others? Did Lady Luck seem more jealous or afraid of Faith?
3. When Faith said that "someone" was "really laying it on thick," she never said who! How likely is it that she was talking about Thomas? Share your thoughts.

The
WordPlay®
Version

*Experience *Instant Replay Bible Study*, seeing how each scripture animates this new story below! Follow along with your own Bible or with our *Scripture Index*. Have Fun!

A Maze In Grace (The Parable)

It's the amusement park's most popular attraction: *The Giant Maze*. And children run inside this life-sized mystery, knowing that only one child has ever completed it **(I Corinthians 9:24) (Matthew 7:14)**! Long ago the whole park watched Justin amaze a maze and become that child legend who found its path to victory **(Psalms 16:11)**. Remembering the only one who's ever won keeps *The Giant Maze* filled with kids vowing to be the second **(Isaiah 35:8) (Psalms 118:20)**.

Still dizzy from her last rollercoaster ride is Little Gracie. She leans on the maze's Start sign, waiting to get her balance back **(Ephesians 6:13)**. Plotting to win **(I Corinthians 9:25)**, Little Gracie stares inside *The Giant Maze's* scenery where everything appears black-and-white **(Deuteronomy 29:29)**. But somehow its players look even dizzier than her! Children inside go from just wondering to just wandering **(I Corinthians 2:8)**. And some players, ashamed of their previous decisions, begin to trace the path of others to manipulate blame **(Matthew 15:14)**. Others just 'go wherever the wind blows' them **(I Corinthians 9:26)**, while some players stand still around its 'gray areas.' Little Gracie is now less dizzy and more concerned as players are losing more than the game. They're losing their energy, their since of direction, and their friendships. She can see clearly, from the Start, this maze is finishing players; not the other way around.

As the game goes on, players can only find the path to frustration. It's *everywhere* as some become aggressive, step on the backs of others (**Proverbs 14:31**), and hit the walls. Also unethical paths have some craftier players even pretend to be Justin, the only winner so far, so they can sell 'the winning directions' to others for their tokens (**Jeremiah 23:16**). And only Grace sees them sneaking away past her and the *Start* area before their kid customers realize they've been cheated (**Matthew 24:11**). And as players begin accusing others for being in their way and blocking their path, Grace drops her head in disappointment.

"It's just a *GAME*!" Grace yells to her school friends inside (**Acts 26:18**).

Grace throws her cotton candy to distract the emotions inside this life-size puzzle (**Ephesians 1:17**). But she misses her target and strikes the 'the man upstairs' operating the *Ferris Wheel*.
"Sorry!" Little Gracie apologizes.
"It's okay," the smiling Park Operator says while climbing down to return her treat. "I couldn't help but notice you starring into *The Giant Maze*. Do you think you'll go inside?"
"I was gonna," Little Gracie says, "but I probably won't. I'm not sure I can win this game. But I am sure this game isn't worth winning (**Ecclesiastics 7:25**)."

"Wow," the Park Operator reacts, "you sound just like Justin!"

Grace pauses, looking up at the Park Operator as he continues (**I Corinthians 12:8**).

"Players don't enter in this maze, as much as this maze enters in its players (**Genesis 6:5**) (**Proverbs 4:23**)! It is here where the lost *pretend* to be found, Grace. It is right *here* where artificial barriers, excuses, rules, and bad reasoning are made (**II Timothy 2:5**). I see too many kids follow everything *except* their heart until they can barely find themselves (**Mark 7:21**)! Wisdom realizes it is, as you say, a game that's not worth winning."

"But Justin *did* win!"

"Uh huh… he sure did," smiles the Park Operator as Grace ponders to herself (**Psalms 15:1**) (**Galatians 2:2**).

"*OOOH*… I've GOT it," Gracie says and runs quickly in a determined direction (**Psalms 15:2**).

The park operator heads back upstairs and hears the whole park cheering. Already knowing why, he turns to see Grace running down the maze's *Finish* with every park light flashing (**II Timothy 4:7**). He smiles. With microphones in her face, Grace thanks 'the man upstairs (**Psalms 140:13**)' and begins to speak (**Acts 20:24**).

"The maze *itself* is the *REAL* barrier (**Hebrews 12:1**)! We simply must go *around* it to find the path to victory! Any other way is a trap for our energy, our growth, and our potential."

The exhausted players lean in closer as Grace continues.

"And for those already inside, the correct way is the only direction this maze doesn't offer: up! So make contact with 'the man upstairs (**II Timothy 2:22**).' He has the Ferris (fairest) way to guide us (**Proverbs 3:6**)' and take us from being lost in a maze, to being found in amazement… above and beyond this game."
The End

Story Symbolism

- Amusement Park = Earth
- Ferris (Fairest) Wheel = Heavenly Viewpoint
- Maze = Politics
- Barriers = Barriers
- Gray Areas = Controversy
- Players = Mankind
- Rollercoaster = Life's Ups and Downs
- Cotton Candy = Good Intentions
- Park Operator = God
- Little Gracie = Grace of God
- Justin = God's Glory
- Black and White Scenery = Alleged Easy Nature
- Fair Tokens = Money and Possessions

Moral

Life is a treasure hunt for smiles inside a pretty tricky maze. But with a little help for 'the man upstairs' you have "a maze in grace (*Amazing Grace*)." And the (narrow) path to victory awaits. Obstacles are rarely in the heart of the maze, but in the maze of the heart.

Share Your Thoughts
Is this parable your favorite?
Vote on our site!

Fun Facts
- Despite her dizziness and disappointment, Little Gracie was an "observer" the entire time (Proverbs 4:7) (Daniel 11:35) and literally from the very Start.
- Inspired by words of the Park Operator, Little Gracie literally "took those steps to win."
- Gracie's outcry that "it's *just* a *GAME*" wasn't enough to distract the "chaos inside." But her victory was.
- Child legend, Justin, is from the *Parable of The Hidden Smile* (in the first *Christian Parables* book) which animated a lesson in Salvation.

Discussion Questions
1. Do you think friendships in jeopardy gave Little Gracie extra motivation to win? Why or why not?
2. Initially "dizzy," Little Gracie waited as long as she needed "to get her balance back" from the (ups-and-downs) rollercoaster ride. How important was her decision?
3. Do you think *The Giant Maze's* black-and-white scenery (alleged easy nature) prevented its players from using their knowledge and wisdom?

The
WordPlay®
Version

*Experience *Instant Replay Bible Study*, seeing how each scripture animates this new story below! Follow along with your own Bible or with our *Scripture Index*. Have Fun!

The Parable of Ice-Cream Soup

"Wish me luck Mom," Faith says through her ice cream tasting. "When Dad arrives home, I'm gonna ask him for a bigger allowance (**Matthew 21:22**)."

"Good for you," Mom replies. "Do you think it might mean more chores for you to do?"

"I *hope* not," Faith replies, starring in her ice cream bowl. "I don't want *more* work! But I'm sure when Dad senses my excitement (**John 16:24**), and sees my '*please* face (**Hebrews 11:6**)', it will be all I need to make this happen (**Mark 11:22**)!"

"I see," Mom says smiling. "Well it's a good thing dishwashing is already a chore of yours (**John 14:15**)! Are you ready?"

"Can I please finish my ice-cream first?"

"Well… why don't you put it in the oven for later?"

"But Mom… the oven is powered *ON* right now! My ice cream will turn to *soup*!"

Mom smiles at Faith and replies, "Always remember the lesson in this moment. Faith *without* works is like ice cream in an oven: only one power-switch away from having artificially warm feelings which surely melt the 'Rocky Road' *before* you finish."

The End

Story Symbolism

- Faith = Confidence
- Oven = Warm Feeling
- Dishes = Obedience
- Mom = Advisor
- Sunny = Believer
- Ice Cream = Desire
- Chores = Works
- Allowance = Blessing
- Dad = Heavenly Father

Moral

A desire cannot be held too long inside initially warm feelings (John 2:14). Like ice cream in an oven, faith without works just melts away until 'solid' action is taken.

Share Your Thoughts

Is this parable your favorite?
Vote on our site!

Fun Facts

- The "Rocky Road" symbolizes both a flavor and a common pathway to a substantial blessing.
- Faith could see the "power-switch" on the oven, but not in herself.
- The dynamic of "daddy's little girl" represents the already pleasing dynamic between (actual) Faith and God (Hebrews 11:6).
- The Mom's smiles represent a natural version of a "warm feeling," rather than artificial development.
- "Ice cream" has a homonym effect with "I scream:" an emotional destiny to unfulfilled desires.

Discussion Questions

1. How do you feel about the "wish me luck" statement Faith began with? What about her reply "I hope not!" Use scripture to support your reaction?
2. Share a time in your life when you may have metaphorically "stored your ice cream in an oven." What "extra work" could you have added?
3. Share a 'rocky road' with your own faith in your life.

The
WordPlay®
Version

*Experience *Instant Replay Bible Study*, seeing how each scripture animates this new story below! Follow along with your own Bible or with our *Scripture Index*. Have Fun!

The Parable of the Lawyer's Lullaby

The Lawyer invites the firm's Detective into his office.

"I need your help," the Lawyer says. "Could you investigate the courtroom in my last trial? Something weird was going on in there!"

"Sure," the Detective agrees, "what happened?"

"Well every time I tried to cross-examine a witness, they became very sleepy, almost instantly! Some even fell asleep on the stand. And the Judge just let them leave, one by one, cheating me out of getting their testimony."

"Wait-a-second," the Detective replies, "maybe *THAT* was the *motive*! Without your evidence, the case would have to be dismissed, right? Are you sure the witnesses were *really* asleep? Maybe they were just pretending to be for a creative escape (**Isaiah 29:15**)."

"You know what," the Lawyer's agrees, "I was in the same courtroom and I was *never* sleepy!"

"And you said the Judge simply excused them from the witness stand. Maybe the Judge was in on this! How else could this sleeping plan work? *Forget* the courtroom conditions! We should investigate the Judge. What's his name?"

"It was… wow, I'm can't remember right now."

"No problem," the Detective assures. "What about the defendant's name? We can go from that?"

"The defendant's name is…. is in my briefcase. Let me find it for you."

The detective waits as the Lawyer scours his entire office.

"You know what," the Detective interrupts, "your case is so *unique* that I'm sure the courthouse can identify it and help me with the details. I'll head over there now."

"Thank you Detective. I know it's here somewhere. I'll call you with the information."

Arriving at the scene of this sleeping phenomenon, the Detective has the extra challenge of investigating without any names, case numbers, timeframes, or even a specific courtroom! But before he can experience his full dilemma, the Detective sees the Lawyer's briefcase in a room which seems empty, until he hears the sound of someone snoring. It is a female Juror fast asleep in the jury panel.

Stunned at her true sleep mode, the Detective knows there is more to discover. So he awakes the Juror.

"We should move you out this room, Miss. I wanna investigate what's causing everyone here to fall asleep."

"Save your investigation," the Juror responds, "it was the Lawyer (**Malachi 2:17**)."

"The Lawyer?"

"It was the Lawyer's lullaby of a case," The Juror replies through a yawn. "Witness after witness took the stand. And no matter honest, informative, or helpful their testimony was… the lawyer kept asking the same questions over and over again, like they *never* answered (**Isaiah 42:20**) (**Proverbs 18:2**)! And the more exhausted the witness got, the more excited the lawyer became (**Proverbs 14:8**) until the Judge declared a mistrial (**Proverbs 14:7**). It was weird, pointless (**Titus 3:9**), and lot of other things! But the one thing it *wasn't* was coffee."

"I realize the trial is over," the Detective says, "but I'm gonna cross-examine *YOU* now! The Lawyer complained about witnesses falling sleeping *before* he got the chance to question, and not *after* like you describe. Can you explain that?"

"That's not true. But I can still explain this because, when I'm not a Juror, I'm a doctor. And based on the Lawyer's behavior, it's clear he has amnesia."

The Detective's eyes widen as she continues.

"I don't think the Lawyer even *remembers* how repetitive and ineffective he was being, or how rude he was to the Judge (**Proverbs 18:6**). In fact, I'd be surprised he even remembered the Judge's name!"

The Detective's eyes widen more (**John 9:39**).

"I bet all this Lawyer remembers are the mysterious conditions where he didn't get his way… and felt dismissed."

The End

Story Symbolism
- Lawyer (Prosecutor) = Reasoning
- Detective = Knowledge
- The Firm = Heart
- Courtroom = Conversation
- Witnesses = Clarity
- Sleepiness = Weariness (Spiritual Exhaustion)
- Briefcase = Bible
- Juror = Truth
- Case = Argument
- Judge = God Almighty
- Lawyer's Condition = Dismissive Behavior

Moral
Strife changes the Truth for itself. Peace changes itself for the Truth. Any "condition" that exhausts the process of knowledge itself can only be the beginning of a "cycle" of unproductive embarrassment and even more mystery.
Don't be "a lawyer with amnesia." If we don't change our absence of mind, then we don't mind our absence of change.

Share Your Thoughts
Is this parable your favorite?
Vote on our site!

Fun Facts

- This entire court story never mentioned a defendant, but only "something weird going on."
- Both the Lawyer and the Detective shared the same firm(ness), with initial reflexes toward each other (Proverbs 21:2).
- The Detective's discovery, without any real details, symbolizes the promise: seek and you shall find (Jeremiah 29:13).
- The case was officially declared a mistrial (temporary); it was not dismissed (final) (Matthew 3:2).

Discussion Questions

1. How would you rate the interrogation level of the Detective toward other characters?
2. What other reasons are possible for why the Detective was willing to begin an investigation with "an extra challenge" of no real details? Share a similar story where someone's determination skipped the details like the Detective.
3. How different would the story have been if the Detective were never called in?

Character Interaction

What kind of skills would a detective need to have to investigate without any details, like this one? Read the Detective's *Charity versus Ability* essay and "discover" 3 essential things to be effective in any "case (Chapter 4)!"

The
WordPlay®
Version

*Experience *Instant Replay Bible Study*, seeing how each scripture animates this new story below! Follow along with your own Bible or with our *Scripture Index*. Have Fun!

Peculiar Treasure (The Parable) (Poetry)

No man exists with my enchanted wish
to craft a love affair with God and trust His management,
and graph above the stares I've gotten from abandonment
But yet, I couldn't understand it when HE granted this!
(II Corinthians 5:5) (Ephesians 1:13)

Imagine this: God said, "Enough repairs! You must be fair
(Ephesians 4:30).
Prepare MY coming from upstairs
to interrupt these prayers.
From your heart, the truth is clever
But putting these clues together….
gives you your measure of 'peculiar treasure.'
I have merged your truth with pleasure many years ago.
I have blurred you views in pressure.
Any tear would know!
You empty fears should show exactly how,
so don't attack ME now…"
Then HE appeared in those attracting clouds **(John 15:26)**.

With all my prayers that last for paragraphs,
I didn't dare to ask a thing except to spare the laugh
and share the facts
I said, "I'm ready for the clues you'll part with."

God replied, "How shall I start this
to prove your heart rich?
I have evidence, Heaven sent, of your enchanted wish.
It has a puzzle-tested smile (**Isaiah 11:2**)
that's left your struggle less than mild (**John 14:26**).
The first to dance with
in your circumstances (**Romans 8:9**),
It's like a Couple blessed with child,
within one huddle-essence style (**Galatians 5:22-23**)!
Still guessing? It was my blessing to your urgent request.
And Mother Nature's still requesting a paternity test
(**John 14:17**).
'Cause who'd believe the Earth could surface this
(**John 3:8**)?
Somehow your birth certificate goes perfect with this wish.

But only hear It when you listen in (**I Corinthians 2:13**),
for a rest above words (**Romans 8:26**).
The Holy Spirit is my synonym
for 'Heaven on Earth (**II Corinthians 3:17**).'
So when I bless a fellow Christian
to digest My Melo System ... (**I Corinthians 6:19**)
It proves your measure of peculiar treasure.... forever
(**Romans 15:13**)."
The End

*In no way is this parables use of "peculiar treasure"
intended to compete with or replace the original reference
to Israelites in Exodus. It is merely symbolic of an equal
since of appreciation in the "new" temple of the New
Testament.

Poetry Symbolism
- Man = Christians
- Enchanted Wish = Oneness with God
- Peculiar Treasure = The Holy Spirit
- Upstairs = Heaven

Moral
No one can afford to overlook our current spiritual shepherd: The Holy Spirit. Ever since Jesus rose again, our Leader is so close to us… that It's *inside* us! And It's influence is so overwhelming that even the world acknowledges it through other nicknames (like Conscience). So during our spiritual journey to the New Testament's "Promised Land (Heaven)," in this wilderness of a world, look no further for a sign. Look inside! God Bless.

Share Your Thoughts
Is this parable your favorite?
Vote on our site!

Fun Facts
- The man was unknowingly interacting with and through his "enchanted wish" the entire time (John 15:26)!
- Notice that God respected the man's request to "spare the laugh and share the facts."
- The "prayers that last for paragraphs" represent long, lengthy, traditional religious formats.
- Notice the easy-going, one-on-one dynamic the entire time.

- Realize that God actually did come down specifically to talk with the man about a better relationship.

Discussion Questions

1. When God jokingly said "don't attack ME now," what could HE have been making a subtle reference to?
2. Elaborate on the lyrics "…from your heart, the truth is clever."
3. What do you suppose God meant by saying, "Enough repairs?"
4. God respected the man's request to "spare the laugh and share the facts." How unique might this approach be compared to others with God?

The
WordPlay®
Version

*Experience *Instant Replay Bible Study*, seeing how each scripture animates this new story below! Follow along with your own Bible or with our *Scripture Index*. Have Fun!

Batteries Not Included (The Parable)

"Here you go," Corey says dropping his coins into Jeff's hands.

"Sold," Jeff says, "I have more baseball cards for the same price."

"Wow," Corey replies, "even after all the one's you sold at school today, you *still* have some left? What are you saving up for anyway?"

"Come on, the cards are in my room."

"Wow," Corey says walking inside, "you sure have a lot of new batteries lying around in here! You should look for a way to sell *these* instead to afford whatever you... what are you saving up for?"

Tommy ponders how to answer until Chris realizes on his own.

"Wait-a-minute," Chris says, "you sell your baseball cards... to buy all these batteries?"

"Yeah," Jeffrey admits. "It's the only way to keep playing my video game! All these batteries are for this game player."

"Lemme see," Corey picks up this demanding device. "Wait a second! This game player has a chord attached! Just plug it in, silly!"

"Corey, it's too uncomfortable when it's plugged in (**Exodus 20:18-19**)! Who likes being tethered to the wall? I wanna feel further away and able to move around more (**Exodus 20:21**)!"

"So… you're actually *hoping* to 'sell out' your birthday gift of baseball cards (**I Corinthians 12:4**), just to afford your plan to feel *LESS* connected (**James 4:10**)?" Sounds to me like a 'different game' with an 'extra controller (**Matthew 6:24**).'"

Jeff considers this as Corey continues.

"How far away and detached do you need to be inside the comfort of your own home? You're right beside an uninterrupted power source (**Exodus 20:22**), which your Father already paid for (**I Corinthians 7:23**) (**John 3:16**)! Keep the rest of your cards (**Romans 12:6**), keep the quality of your time and play. Stay connected (**I Corinthians 12:27**) (**Exodus 20:20**)."

The End

Story Symbolism
- Home = God's Presence
- Baseball Cards = Gifts & Purpose
- Birthday Gift = Unique Gifts from God
- Sell = Trade (Sacrifice)
- Game Player = Heart
- Video Game = Lifestyle
- Power Source = God
- Batteries = Spiritual Distance
- Chord = Relationship with God

Moral
Direct fellowship with God will perfect the needs of a man's heart. But preferring more (cordless) distance begins a cycle of control and sacrifice of your God-given gifts until you have completely "sold out." Don't be your own Delilah and "cut yourself short." It's too costly for anyone. *"Start over!"*

Share Your Thoughts
Is this parable your favorite?
Vote on our site!

Fun Facts
- The baseball cards symbolize the potential to discover extreme value.
- Jeff's character was inspired by Esau
- Jeff's full first name (Jeffrey) initially sounds "free."
- The moment where Jeff "ponders how to answer" symbolizes rehearsed public opinion.
- Corey's discovery of the chord did not surprise Tommy. He already realized it!

Discussion Questions
1. Despite realizing the chord before Chris, Tommy prefaced his dilemma by insisting the batteries were "the only way to get playing time!" What might his motivation had been?

Character Interaction
Take the *Stay Connected Challenge*
Continue to Chapter 4

*Experience *Instant Replay Bible Study*, seeing how each scripture animates this new story below! Follow along with your own Bible or with our *Scripture Index*. Have Fun!

The Parable of the Waitress's Tip

"Well hello again Eugene," the Waitress approaches. "What will it be today? Your usual lunch special?"

"Well that kinda depends," Eugene replies. "Is it true that you guys are closing early today?

"Yeah," the Waitress confirms, "we'll be closing early right before dinner time."

"I see," Eugene says handing the menu back, "I'll have Combo One… Two… Three-Four-Five and Combo Six…with a Diet Cola please."

"Well if your co-workers are all dining here, you could use our banquet room with a bigger table!"

"No… this is all gonna be for me, just me," Eugene says sadly. "See I've been struggling with something inside me that just never feels full (**John 16:24**)! My appetite mysteriously just keeps on ticking to extra weight, but won't wait extra! So I'll need to eat Dinner for Lunch today too! I apologize, I shouldn't bother you with my problems (**Ecclesiastics 2:17**)."

"That's okay," the Waitress says. "Let me bring you an appetizer immediately. I'll be right back!"

Almost before he can agree, the Waitress returns to his table with the appetizer as promised.

"Thank you, really."

Time goes by without the Waitress in sight. Finally Eugene sees her and gestures urgently.

"Thanks so much for this appetizer so far. But whatever you guys haven't cooked yet, please don't! I can't explain why, but I feel *great* inside with no hunger after that miniature-sized appetizer! And of course I'll gladly pay for..."

"We didn't make any of them," the Waitress smiles. "I knew we wouldn't need too."

"Really," Eugene says surprised, "how?"

"Well... I only work here to put myself through college to become a Nutritionist. So I am educated on the natural way digestion works! The platter I gave you is organic (**John 6:35**) (**Galatians 5:22-23**) (**Psalms 23:5**): free from the artificial preservatives designed to keep people hungry."

"Are you serious? There are ingredients like that?"

"Oh yeah," the waitress sits down with Eugene and whispers, "there are chemicals to make bread rise more attractively (**Luke 12:1**), artificial sweeteners to change energy levels (**I Timothy 5:13**). And unfortunately Eugene, I'm dishing about the dishes *here*! I just found out today that this place uses them."

"So *this* is the reason for my appetite."

"It's also the reason for this place closing early. The Chef quit... right after I did this morning (**Psalms 1:1**)! In fact, I'm not even supposed to be here right now! But I've been hiding around so I can warn my favorite customers."

"I can't thank you enough," Eugene reacts. "Can I pay you for the appetizer?"

"It's on me **(I Thessalonians 5:14) (Isaiah 49:4)**," the Waitress says, "Eugene you're a great and generous customer. So *THIS* time let *me* give *YOU* a tip: since this is the only restaurant in town, start growing your own healthy foods **(Proverbs 12:11)**, and learn how to cook **(Psalms 128:2) (II Timothy 2:15)**. The appetite you once had is *nothing* compared to the appetite of this business. It's like a "bottomless pit **(Proverbs 30:16)**!"

The End

Story Symbolism

- Restaurant = Earth
- Appetite = Purpose
- Hunger = Void in the Heart
- Organic = Natural Intent
- Waitress = Truth
- Eugene = Mankind
- Chef = Compromise
- Artificial Ingredients = Man-made Influence
- Cooking = Bible Study
- Bread Chemical = Leaven of the Pharisees
- Menu = Earthly Satisfaction
- Artificial Sweeteners = Vain Motivation
- Appetizer = Bread of Life & Fruits of Holy Spirit

Moral

There's no appetite to sin around the spiritual "bread" of
life, "fruits" of the Holy Spirit, and a "cup" that runneth
over! Avoid the "aftertaste" of vanity. And always
remember that nothing "serves" a man better than the truth.
God bless!

Share Your Thoughts

Is this parable your favorite?
Vote on our site!

Fun Facts

- Realize the quitting order: first the Waitress (Truth),
  then the Chef (Compromise).
- Eugene's order, without looking at the menu,
  symbolizes that he's "seen it all before."
- The news about the restaurant's early closing
  probably came from "a sign."
- Notice the Waitress reflex to "sit down and whisper
  with" Eugene, when he pursued more knowledge.

Discussion Questions

1. Overall how would you rate the Waitress's
   customer service skills?
2. Why do you think the Waitress responded to
   Eugene's needs first, before offering the bigger
   picture?
3. How do you feel about the Waitress hiding around
   after quitting to warn her favorite customers?
4. Notice how "that's okay" was the Waitress's reply,
   when Eugene felt he shared too much of his
   personal challenges to her. How beneficial was this?

Character Interaction

She's ready to 'dish about those dishes!' After all, the
Waitress no longer works for them anymore, right? As the
Waitress continues hiding around to warn more customers,
you have a unique opportunity to help her spread this
fulfilling message further! Read and share her rhyming
mission as a *Camouflaged Prophet* in Chapter 4. God bless!

The
WordPlay®
Version

*Experience *Instant Replay Bible Study*, seeing how each scripture animates this new story below! Follow along with your own Bible or with our *Scripture Index*. Have Fun!

The Parable of the Counselor's Gift

"It's a gift," the School Counselor explains to the news reporter. And it seems to be her answer to every question, even though *she* asked for this interview. "It's a gift" is all she offers to explain her sudden popularity. Surveys score this School Counselor at number one: more admired than the Principal (**II Timothy 2:10**), the Coach (**II Corinthians 1:6**), and all the teachers combined (**Galatians 3:24**)! The news reporter continues trying for a variety of answers.

"Well what about the scoring pattern, Counselor? I notice you score highest with kids involved in school fights. Could you talk *specifically* about how you inspire them? How do you do it?

The School Counselor does open up more. But her responses seem very basic with nothing unique enough to justify her isolated success. From "let you smile be your umbrella" to "forget your troubles and just get happy," the journalist sits both confused and unimpressed (**Luke 18:7**). His next question probes deeper.

"And despite 'the gift' you have, school fights have *actually* been on the rise (**Proverbs 29:9**)! Now it's actually been suggested that some kids are literally fighting to see you. Some believe their misbehavior is only done to skip the long waiting line to make an appointment with you, Counselor! How do you respond? Or maybe you have a different theory to helps us understand."

"Well I think that *maybe* it's a challenge for me to be even *less* selfish with my gift."

"I see," replies the now frustrated news reporter. "Well... would it be okay, Counselor, to see you in action one day?"

"I'll share my gift, *sure!*"

The next day another school fight occurs (**Proverbs 29:10**). The one-sided battle between an Honor student and his bully increases the crowd and the chaos longer than usual (**Proverbs 17:12**). So the Counselor is desperately called. Live news cameras follow behind them as they walk into the Principals Office.

"Okay," the Counselor says entering inside "where are the boys?"

"We separated them," the secretary answers. "Bully is Room 1, honor student Room 2."

"Thanks." The Counselor turns toward the Reporter. "Okay I *always* deal with the more likely victim first which is the honor student in Room 2. I'll speak to him alone."

"Absolutely!" The news reporter says cuing the cameraman.

As the Counselor heads inside, her school fans eavesdrop next to the door for the magical conversation they expect. But the words they can make out are the same phrases *they* use: "let your smile be your umbrella," and "forget your troubles and just get happy!" Five minutes pass, the door re-opens, and an instantly overjoyed schoolboy walks out.

"Amazing," a fan says. "It truly is a gift!"

The little boy is now even trying to make arraignments to talk with the other boy.

"That's so mature of you young man," another fan says, "but I think the Counselor is first!"
"Actually," The Counselor says, "the security guards are first! It's our school policy to always send them in first to determine if the bigger aggressor is calm enough and I'm safe enough to go in."
"Sure!" the news reporter continues to observe.

Security guards go in and quickly return shaking their heads against it. The Counselor as she head nods back.

"Well it looks like I'm done here," the Counselor says. "We'll all just need to be more patient with the other boy."
"Sure!" The first boy agrees giving her a hug.
"Incredible," the cameraman admits to the reporter.
"Thank you for coming." The counselor says to the news reporter. Pulling him closer, the Counselor whispers in his ear, "I told you… it's a gift."

Applause surrounds the Principals office as she leaves smiling.

Still curious about the increase in school fights, the reporter asks to interview the other boy (**I Thessalonians 5:9**). Immediately the guards fiercely block the door (**Matthew 23:13**). But even quicker are other school officials insisting the entire news team leave. And suddenly the mystery becomes clear to him.

"Oh my…" the reporter runs in the other direction past everyone with his confused cameraman. "I think we have an even *bigger* story."

Rushing to the secretary, the reporter stares in disbelief.

"You *switched* the boys and the rooms!"

The secretary shivers as the crowd develops.

"You *tricked* the Counselor into consoling the *bully*, and ignoring the real victim (**Ecclesiastics 9:16**)! And you used the security guards to block off the right entrance (**Psalms 94:21**)!"

The security guards rush to the exit with their guilt, pushing news cameras away.

"So the *REAL* reason fights keep happening here is because the School Counselor bullies the *guilt* these bullies have developed from their own bullying until it disappears (**Proverbs 17:15**)!"

The crowd stares with the cameras as he continues (**Proverbs 18:5**).

"It's *NOT* a gift! It's a deception that you're causing the Counselor and everyone else to believe (**Proverbs 24:24**)! Oh, you are in big trouble (**Isaiah 5:20**). Someone get me to The Principal!"

"Good luck with that," replies the secretary, "you won't believe this *either* but I was *just* doing my job! And I don't work for HIM. I work for *her*."

The End

Story Symbolism

- School Counselor = Simplicity
- Secretary (Assistant): Manipulation
- News Reporter = Righteousness (Hunger & Thirst)
- School Fights = Strife
- Cameraman = Public Viewpoint
- Survey = Opinions
- The Principal = The Principle of Righteousness
- Teacher - Official Advisors
- School = The World
- Interview - Testing the Spirits
- Gift = Presents (of Presence)
- Honor Student = Wisdom
- Bully = Folly
- Security Guards = Advice
- School Policy = Tradition

Moral

Simplicity is willing to manipulate itself and betray wisdom *just* to be popular (believe it or not). So its mysterious 'gift' that merely sounds like presents (presence) should be fairly questioned (or interviewed). Simplicity is a lukewarm intervention more likely to protect vanity, and block truth. Any authority lacking a real "hunger and thirst for righteousness" will only increase the ongoing struggle between wisdom and folly.

Share Your Thoughts
Is this parable your favorite?
Vote on our site!

Fun Facts
- It was the Counselor who asked for the interview, not the other way around (Proverbs 16:19).
- The Counselor's private whisper animates a reprobate mind (Romans 1:28).
- The (non-questionable) school policy (tradition) was the only thing the Counselor was specific about.
- The eavesdropping fans could not make out any questions (just rhetorical statements).

Discussion Questions
1. Interpret the very last line in the story: "I don't work for HIM, I work for her."
2. What do you think the other boy would have told the news reporter (in scripture)?
3. Imagine how the Counselor's fans felt around the news crew? Explain why.

Character Interaction
No one got a chance to hear from the other boy: the real Honor Student. But you can! Read his essay: *The Top 20 Biblical Signs of a Fool* in Chapter 4.

The
WordPlay®
Version

*Experience *Instant Replay Bible Study*, seeing how each scripture animates this new story below! Follow along with your own Bible or with our *Scripture Index*. Have Fun!

The Parable of the Calendar's Watch

The cheers get louder and louder as the Celebrity walks inside the store. She shakes the business promoter's hand and then waves hers to the cheering crowd: each one with a calendar in their hand. Simply buying this store's calendar today earns an autograph and chance to meet the star in person! And with her fan club of jumping girls and blushing boys, this store has already sold out (**I Peter 4:8**). So the promoter rushes out to make more copies. Meanwhile the cheers follow the Celebrity as she meets, poses for pictures, and finally signs everyone's calendar. But in the corner of her eye, she sees a separate stand with a gentleman selling another product. *Whatever* it is doesn't appear to be doing nearly as well as the calendars (**I Corinthians 13:4**).

"Mark your calendars folks," the promoter announces, "because she, and our wonderful calendars, will be returning back here soon!"

Applause erupts again as the event planners thank her. And as the chasing crowd moves to the left, she gets a much clearer view of the gentleman salesman. Still trying to make out exactly what product he's selling, she leaves for lunch.

Inside the restaurant with her agent, the Celebrity notices people in her VIP section disappear, running toward a new arriving guest. She realizes it's the same less popular gentleman vendor at the marketplace event. The older gentleman hands out the same mysterious product to all who simply ask. And to the Celebrity's surprise, she realizes that even her agent has left their table to shake the gentleman's hand (**Isaiah 29:19**).

"Just who is this guy?" the Celebrity wonders, "and what is he selling?" The gentleman smiles at her stare and whispers an equally mysterious request in her agent's ear. And filled with excitement, her agent takes his hand and walks the gentleman to the Celebrity's table.

"I'm a huge fan of you." The gentleman says to the Celebrity.
"I really appreciate it," the Celebrity replies looking around for his calendar copy to autograph. "Thank you sir!"
"I was just talking with your agent, hoping you would consider endorsing *my* product instead of Mr. Calendar's (**Romans 11:14**)."
"Oh ... we *ACCEPT!*" The agent says impulsively (**I Peter 1:22**).
"Well *wait*-a-second," the Celebrity laughs along with the gentleman. "I would like to know more if I may!"
"Of course (**Matthew 11:29**)!" The gentleman says sincerely.
"Please have a seat, sir!"
"Here take *my* chair, Sir!" The agent offers. "You guys discuss the details while I'll find our waiter for another chair!"

As the gentleman sits down next to her, customers peek with smiles and thumbs up, cheering on the lucky one. It is unclear to the Celebrity which one she is. The gentleman begins.

"I know what Mr. Calendar has agreed to pay you. But I am prepared to offer you even more!"

"Well with all due respect, sir. Your product didn't seem as popular at the store event."

"You can't always believe what you see (**John 9:39**)," the gentleman says smiling. "I own the entire marketplace. Mr. Calendar rented today's limited time here. I was just keeping an eye on my store (**Job 1:7**)."

The Celebrity leans in more as he continues.

"Today's shoppers only see the decorations of a crafty businessman (**II Corinthians 4:4**): celebrity appeal, commercials, and a chance to party with the majority for a price. But the big picture has Mr. Calendar in huge debt (**Romans 6:23**). He secretly needs your endorsement for access to your fans, which means a chance to sell items and be less 'in the red (**Revelation 12:12**).'

"Well how can Mr. Calendar afford *me* then?"

"He can't! Mr. Calendar put tricks in your contract to avoid paying you."

The Celebrity's begins to remember her contract's complicated language (**II Corinthians 2:11**).

"But his business tactics go even further (**I Peter 5:8**)!" The gentleman points to the Celebrity's sample calendar. "Look closer at his calendar that everyone bought today. Do you see anything odd about it?"

"Oh my goodness!" the Celebrity says while pointing, "It's *LAST* year's calendar!"

"That's right. Mr. Calendar is all about the money even when it means deliberately selling items that are worthless and outdated with no real value **(Isaiah 3:9)**. He uses your fans' appetite to meet you as camouflage."

The Celebrity's eyes open almost a wide as her fans after seeing her.

"We've got to do something, Sir! Some people are living according to that outdated material."

"For all his offenses, I will to drive him out soon. But right now I am more concerned about the unsuspecting customers **(Romans 11:15)**."

"Well if it's *your* business, what are you waiting for, sir? You could do it right now."

"For the customers' sake, the real competition is between his craftiness and my truth. And this is exactly the message I would like you to share while endorsing my *free* product. Mr. Calendar won't be able to compete."

"Why… is your product a calendar too?"

"My product is *SO* much better than a calendar **(James 5:20) (I Peter 4:7)**."

"So let me get this straight," the Celebrity clarifies. "You want to hire me for a celebrity endorsement of your *free* product: a product that you believe will somehow put Mr. Calendar out of business because, in your opinion, your product satisfies *BETTER* than a calendar! What is this product you created?"

"It's called eternal life."

The End

Moral
Sin is about as cheap and outdated as a Clearance Sale on last year's calendar. Buy Eternal Life, freely given by God's grace. The children of God are like anointed celebrities appealing to the heart of man. The real celebration is salvation. Start spreading the news!

Share Your Thoughts
Is this parable your favorite?
Vote on our site!

Story Symbolism
- The Celebrity = *You!*
- The Gentleman = God
- Agent = Heart
- Crowd = Mankind
- Fans = Family and Friends (of You)
- Event = Life
- Calendar = Sin (For a Season)
- Store = Earth
- Restaurant = Spiritual Realm
- Endorse = Live For
- Autograph = Proclaim
- Mr. Calendar = Satan
- Payment = Blessing
- Contract = Supernatural Intentions
- Restaurant Staff = Angels
- Rented Time = Earthy Time for a Season

Fun Facts

- No one ate at the table while the gentleman spoke, unless you count "HIS every word (Matthew 4:4)."
- The Celebrity first view of the gentleman at the store was from the "right" angle.
- The agent (heart) demonstrated the same fan club setting for the Gentlemen (God).
- The excitement of the agent (heart) caused behavior out of traditional character, as it should.
- The whisper into the agent's ear represents the privacy between God's voice and his children.
- The gentleman's "smile at her stares" represents the God's reaction to anyone seeking his face.
- Notice the gentleman never actually had a calendar himself (pure, without sin).
- The gentleman referred to their setting as "my" restaurant, in addition to the marketplace he owns.
- The owner was against a full monopoly.
- The gentleman being patient with his intervention was ultimately to protect the naïve customers from the effect of a riot.
- The gentleman adjusted himself to the Celebrity's auditioning norms before showing her the big picture.
- Not one episode of envy centered around the restaurant.
- The customers at the restaurant symbolize "new creatures" being served (still competing to serve God).
- The gentleman beginning statement, "I'm a huge fan of you," animates how God loved us first.

- The gentleman did not speak competitively; he only spoke truthfully.

Discussion Questions

1. When has your own "agent (heart)" been moved toward the gentleman (God) almost independently out of natural excitement, like in the story? Share this moment.
2. If The Gentleman claimed his success was self-made by his "blood, sweat, and tears," which scripture(s) supports this.
3. How do you feel about the gentleman's stating "the real competition is between his craftiness and my truth?"

Character Interaction

The story never mentioned what The Celebrity is famous *for*! She is a musical communicator (Rapper). But now, with her new endorsement deal, she is a new and improved Christian Rapper. Experience her uplifting lyrics in *Perception Bearer* in Chapter 4. Have fun!

The
WordPlay®
Version

*Experience *Instant Replay Bible Study*, seeing how each scripture animates this new story below! Follow along with your own Bible or with our *Scripture Index*. Have Fun!

Couples Therapy Parable (Poetry)

Past his years of mixing wrath with tears
and wedding rings,
none of his tactics cleared the atmosphere
(**Proverbs 29:18**).
And everything that's happened here is obvious
I follow this, as their psychologist,
reluctant to acknowledge this scene:
A narcissistic groom, it seems (**Proverbs 16:18**),
their heart logistics doomed (**Luke 14:11**) if we
can't quickly earn some apologies (**Mark 1:15**)
As their exes cheer against them (**John 10:10**),
and their kid's the clearest victim (**I John 3:16**),
let us learn from analogies (**Matthew 13:13**).

Story Symbolism

- Couple = God & Mankind
- Kid = Jesus
- Narcissism = Pride
- Exes = Lucifer, Fallen Angels
- Psychologist = The Holy Spirit
- Apologies = Repentance
- Wedding Rings = Covenants
- Tactics = Non-direct Strategy

Moral

There's always a *U* and *I* in "communication." But the distance varies by perception! Therefore, it is so important to find a common denominator (like parables) when relaying to one another, both in and out The Kingdom.

Share Your Thoughts

Is this parable your favorite?
Vote on our site!

Fun Facts

- The pride is followed by the words "it seems," suggesting that maybe unawareness is the root of the problem.
- The "narcissistic groom (it seems)" character is interchangeable between God and Man since they share the same image (Genesis 1:26) (but of course this describes Man).
- Although the urgency was to "earn some apologies," the ultimate goal was to rebuild the relationship.

Discussion Questions

1. How do you interpret the phrase "mixing wrath with tears?"
2. What might the fact that "none of his tactics cleared the atmosphere" reveal about the groom (mankind)?

The
WordPlay®
Version

*Experience *Instant Replay Bible Study*, seeing how each scripture animates this new story below! Follow along with your own Bible or with our *Scripture Index*. Have Fun!

The Parable of the Blindfold

Thomas tilts with his telephone in the early morning, preparing to leave a message.

"Yes *hello…* I'm a patient at *The Lucky Ones Clinic*. And I need to cancel my appointment today with my doctor, Lady Luck. Something came up (**Psalms 118:8**). But I have enough of your *4-Leaf-Clover* cream to last me until we can reschedule. Thanks! Bye."

Thomas drops the phone next to a map he is still starring at, along with a business card he kept (**Proverbs 3:5**), matching the addresses (**Proverbs 3:6**). And practically tip-toeing to his car, Thomas proceeds out of town to the new destination.

"Hi," a hospital clerk greets Thomas as he arrives inside, "can I help you sir?"
"Yes good morning! I'm Thomas Walker and have an appointment with Doctor Powers."
"Sure! Please follow me to the office."
Thomas continues to look around ensuring he's not noticed by anyone from his town.
"Good morning," the new doctor walks inside, "is it Thomas Walker?"

"Doctor Powers," Thomas says shaking her hand. "Thanks for agreeing see me."

"My pleasure (**II Corinthians 1:24**). But we're on a first name basis here. Please just call me Faith."

"You got it! Faith, I heard about you through my friend Christian. She tells me you're the best!"

"Well it's *actually* a team effort," Faith smiles. "Let's make it your turn to feel better! How can I help?"

"Well my skin type is extremely sensitive to sunlight. And I live in a desert, with no real way to block it! Until I can afford to move, I've been using a medicated *4-Leaf-Clover* cream to lessen the effects."

"Wow," Faith says, "someone must have to really 'lay it on thick!'"

"Yeah, my original doctor does. It helps a little, but it's really expensive! And she insists it's the only way! So I guess I'm here for a second opinion."

"Sure," Faith replies, "let's run some tests and I think I can help you with that."

Much to the surprise of Thomas, Faith actually begins by checking his blood pressure.

"Oh this is good news!" Faith says, "Thomas I'm happy to offer you a cheaper and better alternative. Based on these tests, your condition actually needs *physical* therapy, not medicated creams. And, if you like, we can begin right now!"

"Absolutely!"

"So let's head to my operating room. And, for this to work, I'll need to blindfold you first (**Hebrews 11:1**). Then I'll take your hand and lead you inside a machine where you'll vary your speeds when I tell you to. Are you ready?"

Although unsure how this will help, Thomas submits. Faith begins her unique procedure.

Time passes by unnoticed as Thomas awakes from a deep sleep. And he finds himself somehow back inside his bed at home! But before he can call this whole experience a dream, Thomas notices a doctor's note signed by Faith (**Romans 10:17**). But as he holds it up to the window to read it, no sunlight shines through. In fact there's no heat to be felt either! Puzzled, Thomas turns on a lamp. And he immediately notices his incredibly smooth, cooled, healthy skin.

"Oh my!" Thomas drops the letter and runs to his mirror. He looks completely revitalized and renewed. But along with his image reflection, he sees a new, giant object outside his window. Turning around, Thomas finally realizes what has happened: somehow a mountain has moved to block the sunlight from the house, forever protecting his skin condition (**II Timothy 4:7**).

After hours of pinching himself and crying tears of joy, Thomas returns to Faith's note:

'Keep the rest of these mustard seeds, Thomas.
Doctor's orders!'
To Be Continued

*Stand firm with Faith as this parable continues and Faith is tested!

Story Symbolism

- Lady Luck = Superstitions, Myths
- Dr. Faith Powers = Faith
- (Doubting) Thomas = Mankind
- Business Card = Change
- Map = Mind State
- Prescriptions = Insistence
- Desert = Deserted Place
- Christian = Fellowship
- Skin = Potential
- Sunlight = Exposure to Doubt
- Physical Therapy = Action

Moral, *Discussion Questions*, & *Fun Facts* revealed after full story*

The Blindfold Parable 2: Testing Faith

Thomas holds up the remaining mustard seeds, literally cool enough to wonder if he'll ever need the *4 Leaf Clover* cream again. Perhaps Faith knew was she was doing after all, though Thomas couldn't determine how. As he keeps pondering how, his phone rings.

"Hello?" Thomas answers.

"Good afternoon! I'm Katelyn with the *Good News Team*, preparing you in advance that we'll be doing a story on the miracle in your town. Did you by chance witness any of while it was happening? Could we interview you?"

"I did not witness it. But I think I know how it happened! Please come over."

Moments later the doorbell rings.

"Coming," Thomas yells while adjusting his best tie.

He tried calling Faith, but couldn't reach her. He retrieves the business card that started it all. And as he arrives, he opens his door to another memory.

"Oh...Lady Luck." Thomas reacts, "I didn't know you made house calls! I appreciate it but right now's not a good t... **(I Corinthians 16:13)**"

"She's not a *real* doctor, Thomas! Faith is a fraud."

"How did you know that..."

"I *saw* you go in her office, okay." Lady Luck explains while massaging her rabbit's foot. "Luckily, I was 'at the right place at the right time,' Thomas. I came to take you back to *The Lucky Ones Clinic* and hopefully undo whatever Faith did."

"Are you kidding?" Thomas replies, "With all due respect, the way Faith works is more effective (**Ephesians 6:16**). Before I even *knew* this mountain was moved, I rested better. I didn't just sit still and let everyone 'rub it in,' I finally got up (**James 1:3**)! I *walked* with Faith (**II Corinthians 5:7**)."

"And when you walked with Faith…. I bet you were blindfolded."

"I was," Thomas replies in curiosity. "Why?"

"Well," Lady Luck laughs, "let me show you what you didn't see as you walked blindly with Faith in another room, increasing your speed."

Lady Luck hands Thomas a picture of him blindfolded at Faith's office, on a treadmill.

"How can this be real?" Thomas says through embarrassment.

"I *told* you she's a con-artist! Why is this so… oh I see! You thought Faith moved this mountain?"

Laughter increases in Lady Luck, as Thomas sees the *Good News Team* arriving for an interview.

"Hey," Lady Luck grabs Thomas arm, "this town's not big enough for *two* doctors. So if you even mention Faith to them, I'll embarrass you with these pictures and your gullible story."

Thomas runs emotionally past everyone and into his car, to everyone's surprise (**I Peter 5:9**). Driving off quickly, he can still feel the laugher from Lady Luck and all who she might tell. Once again, Thomas retrieves the business card and drives even more intently than before.

Walking past the secretary, and into Faith's procedure room, Thomas looks around and the true account of a treadmill.

"Thomas," Faith walks in, "is everything okay?"
"How could you play with my feelings like this?"
"What are you talking about?"
"I *trusted* you!"
"Yeah… and you're condition has improved, Thomas! You are making a… *molehill* out of a mountain (**I Thessalonians 3:7**)!"
"So… it's true?" Thomas clarifies. "*You* moved that mountain? How? And why did you need me to embarrass myself by moving around on a treadmill?"
"Thomas let me show you." Faith says pulling out the familiar blindfold. "Perception contaminates the procedure! The challenge is not me shielding this place from you; it is me shielding you from *THIS* place. You don't need thick-skin when you're not exposed."

Thomas continues to listen.

"As for the *physical* therapy? Well… we had to get your heart pumping (**I Corinthians 2:5**), at least long enough to move past your 'doubting, Thomas!' And we had to work together. Remember when I told you this is a team effort? We needed each other's energy (**Ephesians 2:8**). And apparently it was enough for you to work with!"

"What do you mean by 'enough for me to work with?"

"Oh ye of little faith," The doctor smiles, "I didn't move that mountain. *You* did! (**I John 5:4**)"

The End

Moral

Faith is a biblically-approved, blindfolded journey within the spiritual rights we have as God's children. And the celebration belongs to the "team effort" between the grace of God and the willingness of Christians to walk with it. Faith is a process too amazing to be confused with luck.

Share Your Thoughts

Is this parable your favorite?
Vote on our site!

Story Symbolism

- Lady Luck = Superstitions, Myths
- The Clinic = Challenges
- Dr. Faith Powers = Faith
- (Doubting) Thomas = Mankind
- Business Card = Change
- Map = Mind State
- Prescriptions = Insistence
- Desert = Deserted Place
- Christian = Fellowship
- Skin = Potential
- Sunlight = Exposure to Doubt
- Physical Therapy = Action
- Treadmill = Obstacles
- Good News Team = Joyful Testimony

Fun Facts

- The words "doubting" and "Thomas" appear together toward the story's end, mentioning the disciple "Doubting Thomas."
- The mustard seeds left by Dr. Faith attribute the biblical process (Matthew 17:20)
- The doctor's full name (Faith Powers) is designed like an incomplete sentence. It is "a team effort" with mankind.
- Lady Luck had her "practice" as a doctor in the desert (deserted place) where Thomas lived.
- As Thomas explained his predicament to Faith, his statement that he couldn't afford to "move" is a double meaning.
- When Faith said that "someone" was "really laying it on thick," she never said who!

Discussion Questions

1. How did you (or your listeners) feel when the picture of the treadmill was revealed? Share a story of your own when your faith was tested.
2. Why do you suppose Lady Luck followed her doubts in Faith with a threat to embarrass Thomas if he mentioned her to others? Did Lady Luck seem more jealous or afraid of Faith?
3. When Faith said that "someone" was "really laying it on thick," she never said who! How likely is it that she was talking about Thomas? Share your thoughts.

The
Family Skit
Version

Play Script Version
Lights-Camera-Action... starring *YOU!*
Scripts your Scripture with no Versus of Verses!

- Lights (Genesis 1:3)
- Camera (Matthew 3:17)
- Action (Mark 16:15)

For family, friends, and fellowship

The
Family Skit
Version

Need More Scripts?
Become the bible lesson, rehearsing with family & friends through Kindle at a discount, and with less paper! Have fun.

The Thirsty Cup Parable
The Importance of Bible Study

Characters:
- Frank: A young schoolboy giving a boost to his friend Christian.
- Christian: the younger boy experiencing the water fountain.
- Narrator: Presenter and Symbolism Host

Props Needed: (stacks of pillows)

Setting:
A school area, directly next to a high water fountain.

Begin Script:

Frank & Christian
(set themselves up for Frank to give Christian a boost over the water fountain)

Narrator:
To reach the top of the water fountain, the thirsty schoolboys work together.

Frank:
I'll lift you on the count of three.

Frank & Christian:
(count together)

One... Two... THREE!

(Frank lifts Christian up)

Narrator:
Frank holds his friend Christian up, with all his child strength, and can hear the water now flowing.

Frank:
Hurry up Christian!

Narrator:
The seconds are getter heavier.

Frank:
Is our cup almost full?

Christian:
(feels puzzled at the word 'cup')

What cup?

Frank:
The big cup we got from the cafeteria... to save for later.
You're not even thirsty right now (Psalms 143:5)!

Christian:
But this way, I will continue to feel full (James 1:22).

Frank:
Forget using your mouth to feel full! Use your cup for a full
fill (Deuteronomy 11:18) (Proverbs 7:3) (Psalms 77:10:11)
(Jonah 2:7)!

Narrator:
Christian's 'weight' becomes too much for Frank to hold,
causing them both to fall (Ecclesiastics 12:1).

Frank:
(gently and safely drops Christian [into stacks of pillows])

Christian:
Sorry Frank!

(motions an offer to lift Frank now)

Narrator:
As Christian tries to return the favor, he is simply not strong enough to lift his friend up.

The End

(Present *Story Symbolism* and *Moral*)

Story Symbolism
- Cafeteria = Wisdom
- Fountain = Bible
- Christian = Christians
- Lift = Support
- Drink = Experience
- Water = Scriptures
- Thirsty = Troubled
- Cup = Heart

Moral
Frank(ly) to every Christian, how can a "cup runneth over" if we drink directly from the faucet? Wisdom is feeling (and filling) the Word in your heart (both are needed). And you'll never urgently "thirst" for biblical instruction.

Share Your Thoughts
Is this parable your favorite?
Vote on our site!

Character Interaction
The good news, for both Christian and Frank, is the sound of their much taller friend walking down that same hall.

And that person is you! Can you them fill their cup? Can you store 20 scriptures? Take *Christian's Challenge!*

Here's how: Visit www.ChristianParables.com and print a free bible trivia copy of *Christian's Challenge.* Good luck.

Instant Replay Bible Study
Scripture Index

Psalms 143:5
I remember the days of old; I meditate on all Your works. I muse on the work of Your hands.
James 1:22
But be doers of The Word, and not hearers only, deceiving yourselves.
Deuteronomy 11:18
Therefore you shall lay up these words of mine in your heart and in your soul, and bind them as a sign on your hand, and they shall be as frontlets between your eyes.
Proverbs 7:3
Bind them on your fingers; write them on the tablet of your heart.
Psalms 77:10-11
And I said, "This is my anguish; but I will remember the years of the right hand of the Most High." I will remember the works of the LORD; Surely I will remember Your wonders of old.
Jonah 2:7
"When my soul fainted within me, I remembered the LORD. And my prayer went up to You, into Your holy temple.

Ecclesiastics 12:1
Remember now your Creator in the days of your youth, before the difficult days come, and the years draw near when you say, "I have no pleasure in them."

The
Family Skit
Version

Need More Scripts?
Become the bible lesson, rehearsing with family & friends through Kindle at a discount, and with less paper! Have fun.

A Maze In Grace (The Parable)

It's the most popular 3-D maze challenge for Little Gracie.

Characters

- Little Gracie: A young roller-coaster-loving girl peeking into the park's newest attraction
- Park Operator: the inspiring 'man upstairs' operating the *Ferris Wheel*
- Narrator: Presenter and Symbolism Host
- Children Extras: children moving throughout the maze

Setting

An amusement park with a 3D giant maze for children.

Begin Script

Children Extras:
(run and explore the whole maze in all different directions as the Narrator continues)

Narrator:
(points to the maze)

It's the amusement park's most popular attraction: The Giant Maze. And children run inside this life-sized mystery, knowing that only one child has ever completed it (I Corinthians 9:24) (Matthew 7:14)!

Long ago the whole park watched a kid named Justin amaze a maze and become that child legend who found its path to victory (Psalms 16:11).

Remembering the only one who's ever won keeps The Giant Maze filled with kids vowing to be the second (Isaiah 35:8)(Psalms 118:20).

Little Gracie:
(slowly walks toward the maze, leans against it, and stares inside as the Narrator continues)

Narrator:
Still dizzy from her last rollercoaster ride is Little Gracie. She leans on the maze's *Start* sign, waiting to get her balance back (Ephesians 6:13).

Little Gracie:
(appears dizzy while standing)

Narrator:
Plotting to win (I Corinthians 9:25), Little Gracie stares inside The Giant Maze's scenery where everything appears black-and-white (Deuteronomy 29:29). But somehow its players look even dizzier than her!

Children inside go from just wondering to just wandering (I Corinthians 2:8).

Children Extras:
(appear frustrated and lost)

Little Gracie:
(continues to look inside maze at players)

Narrator:
And some players, ashamed of their previous decisions, begin to trace the path of others to manipulate blame (Matthew 15:14). Others just 'go wherever the wind blows' them (I Corinthians 9:26), while some players stand still around its 'gray areas.'

And now Little Gracie is less dizzy and more concerned as players are now losing more than the game. They're losing their energy, their since of direction, and their friendships. Little Gracie can see clearly, from the Start, this maze is finishing players; not the other way around.

Little Gracie:
(looks closer at the maze players)

Narrator:
As the game goes on, most players can only find the path…
to frustration.

Children Extras:
(appear angry against each other.)

Narrator:
And it's everywhere as some become aggressive, step on
the backs of others (Proverbs 14:31), and hit the walls.

Children Extras:
(some begin exchange coins with each other)

Narrator:
Also… the unethical paths chosen have some craftier
players even pretend to be Justin, the only winner so far, so
they can sell 'the winning directions' to others for their
tokens (Jeremiah 23:16).

Little Gracie:
(shakes her head to herself)

Narrator:
Grace watches them sneaking away toward her and the
Start area before their kid customers realize they've been
cheated (Matthew 24:11).

Extras:
(become even angrier toward each other)

Narrator:
And as players begin accusing others for being in their way and blocking their path, Grace drops her head in disappointment.

Little Gracie:
(yells toward the other players)

It's just a *GAME* (Acts 26:18)!

Narrator:
She throws her cotton candy to distract the emotions inside this life-size puzzle (Ephesians 1:17).

Little Gracie:
(throws candy upward hitting the Park Operator)

Narrator:
But Gracie misses her target and strikes the 'the man upstairs' operating the Ferris Wheel.

Little Gracie:
Sorry!

Park Operator:
(smiles)

It's okay!

(smiles like a proud dad and climbs down slowly toward Little Grace) (hands Little Grace her cotton candy back)

I couldn't help but notice you starring into The Giant Maze. Do you think you'll go inside?

Little Gracie:
I was gonna…but I probably won't.

(looks back at the maze)

I'm not sure I can win this game. But I am sure this game isn't worth winning (Ecclesiastics 7:25).

Park Operator:
Wow… you sound just like Justin!

Little Gracie:
(pauses and looks up at the Park Operator [I Corinthians 12:8])

Park Operator:
Players don't enter in this maze, as much as this maze enters in its players (Genesis 6:5) (Proverbs 4:23)!

Little Gracie:
(glances back and forth between the players and the Park Operator as he continues)

Park Operator:
(points at the maze)

It is here where the lost pretend to be found, Grace. It is right here where artificial barriers, excuses, rules, and their reasoning are made (II Timothy 2:5). I see too many kids follow everything except their heart until they can barely find themselves (Mark 7:21)! Wisdom realizes it is, as you say… a game that's not worth winning.

Little Gracie:
Yeah… but Justin did win!

Park Operator:
(smiles at Little Gracie)

Uh huh… he sure did.

Little Grace:
(ponders to herself [Psalms 15:1] [Galatians 2:2])

OH… I've got it!

(runs quickly in a determined direction [Psalms 15:2])(runs away from audience's view)

Park Operator:
(smiles to himself and climbs back up)

Narrator:
The park operator heads back upstairs and hears the whole park cheering.

[APPLAUSE]

Extras:
(stop playing inside the maze to look at Grace)

Little Grace:
(runs behind the maze in a clear pathway to the maze's Finish)

Narrator:
Already knowing why, he turns to see Grace running down the maze's Finish with every park light flashing (II Timothy 4:7). He smiles.

And with microphones in her face, Grace thanks 'the man upstairs (Psalms 140:13)' and begins to speak (Acts 20:24).

Little Grace:
(holds a microphone)

The maze itself is the REAL barrier (Hebrews 12:1)! We simply must go around it to find the path to victory! Any other way is a trap for our energy, our growth, and our potential.

Extras:
(lean in closer as Grace continues)

Little Gracie:
And for those already inside, the correct way is the only direction this maze doesn't offer: up! Make contact with 'the man upstairs (II Timothy 2:22).' He has the Ferris (fairest) way to guide us (Proverbs 3:6)' and take us from

being lost in a maze, to being found in amazement… above and beyond this game.
The End

Story Symbolism
- Amusement Park = Earth
- Ferris (Fairest) Wheel = Heavenly Viewpoint
- Maze = Politics
- Barriers = Barriers
- Gray Areas = Controversy
- Players = Mankind
- Rollercoaster = Life's Ups and Downs
- Cotton Candy = Good Intentions
- Park Operator = God
- Little Gracie = Grace of God
- Justin = God's Glory
- Black and White Scenery = Alleged Easy Nature
- Fair Tokens = Money and Possessions

Moral
Life is a treasure hunt for smiles inside a pretty tricky maze. But with a little help for 'the man upstairs' you have "a maze in grace (Amazing Grace)." And the (narrow) path to victory awaits. Obstacles are rarely in the heart of the maze, but in the maze of the heart.

Share Your Thoughts
Is this parable your favorite?
Vote on our site!

Fun Facts

- Despite her dizziness and disappointment, Little Gracie was an "observer" the entire time (Proverbs 4:7) (Daniel 11:35) and literally from the very *Start*.
- Inspired by words of the Park Operator, Little Gracie literally "took those steps to win."
- Gracie's outcry that "it's just a GAME" wasn't enough to distract the "chaos inside." But her victory was.
- Child legend, Justin, is from the parable of The Hidden Smile (in the first Christian Parables book) which animated a lesson in Salvation.

Discussion Questions

1. Do you think friendships in jeopardy gave Little Gracie extra motivation to win? Why or why not?
2. Initially "dizzy," Little Gracie waited as long as she needed "to get her balance back" from the (ups-and-downs) rollercoaster ride. How important was her decision?
3. Do you think The Giant Maze's black-and-white scenery (alleged easy nature) prevented its players from using their knowledge and wisdom?

Instant Replay Bible Study
Scripture Index

I Corinthians 9:24
Do you not know that those who run in a race all run, but one receives the prize? Run in such a way that you may obtain it.

Matthew 7:14
Because narrow is the gate and difficult is the way which leads to life, and there are few who find it.

Psalms 16:11
You will show me the path of life, In Your presence is fullness of joy. At Your right hand are pleasures forevermore.

Isaiah 35:8
A highway shall be there, and a road. And it shall be called the Highway of Holiness. The unclean shall not pass over it, but it shall be for others. Whoever walks the road, although a fool, shall not go astray.

Psalms 118:20
This is the gate of the LORD. Through which the righteous shall enter.

Ephesians 6:13
Therefore take up the whole armor of God, that you may be able to withstand in the evil day, and having done all, to stand.

I Corinthians 9:25
And everyone who competes for the prize is temperate in all things. Now they do it to obtain a perishable crown, but we for an imperishable crown.

Deuteronomy 29:29
The secret things belong to the LORD our God, but those things which are revealed belong to us and to our children forever, that we may do all the words of this law.

I Corinthians 2:8
Which none of the rulers of this age knew; for had they known, they would not have crucified the Lord of glory.

Matthew 15:14
Let them alone. They are blind leaders of the blind. And if the blind leads the blind, both will fall into a ditch."

I Corinthians 9:26
Therefore I run thus: not with uncertainty. Thus I fight: not as one who beats the air.

Proverbs 14:31
He who oppresses the poor reproaches his Maker. But he who honors Him has mercy on the needy.

Jeremiah 23:16
Thus says the LORD of hosts: "Do not listen to the words of the prophets who prophesy to you.
They make you worthless. They speak a vision of their own heart, not from the mouth of the LORD.

Matthew 24:11
Then many false prophets will rise up and deceive many.

Acts 26:18
To open their eyes, in order to turn them from darkness to light, and from the power of Satan to God, that they may receive forgiveness of sins and an inheritance among those who are sanctified by faith in Me.

Ephesians 1:17
That the God of our Lord Jesus Christ, the Father of glory, may give to you the spirit of wisdom and revelation in the knowledge of Him.

Ecclesiastics 7:25
I applied my heart to know, to search and seek out wisdom and the reason of things, to know the wickedness of folly, even of foolishness and madness.

I Corinthians 12:8
For to one is given the word of wisdom through the Spirit, to another the word of knowledge through the same Spirit.

Genesis 6:5
Then the LORD saw that the wickedness of man was great in the earth, and that every intent of the thoughts of his heart was only evil continually.

Proverbs 4:23
Keep your heart with all diligence. For out of it spring the issues of life.
II Timothy 2:5
And also if anyone competes in athletics, he is not crowned unless he competes according to the rules.
Mark 7:21
For from within, out of the heart of men, proceed evil thoughts, adulteries, fornications, murders…
Psalms 15:1
LORD, who may abide in Your tabernacle? Who may dwell in Your holy hill?
Galatians 2:2
And I went up by revelation, and communicated to them that gospel which I preach among the Gentiles, but privately to those who were of reputation, lest by any means I might run, or had run, in vain.
Psalms 15:2
He who walks uprightly, and works righteousness, and speaks the truth in his heart…
II Timothy 4:7
I have fought the good fight, I have finished the race. I have kept the faith.
Psalms 140:13
Surely the righteous shall give thanks to Your name; the upright shall dwell in Your presence.
Acts 20:24
But none of these things move me; nor do I count my life dear to myself, so that I may finish my race with joy, and the ministry which I received from the Lord Jesus, to testify to the gospel of the grace of God.

Hebrews 12:1

Therefore we also, since we are surrounded by so great a cloud of witnesses, let us lay aside every weight, and the sin which so easily ensnares us, and let us run with endurance the race that is set before us.

II Timothy 2:22

Flee also youthful lusts; but pursue righteousness, faith, love, peace with those who call on the Lord out of a pure heart.

Proverbs 3:6

In all your ways acknowledge Him and He shall direct your paths.

Need More Scripts?
Become the bible lesson, rehearsing with family & friends through Kindle at a discount, and with less paper! Have fun.

The Parable of Ice-Cream Soup

A little girl learns about the conditions of Faith in an unlikely place.

Characters

- Mother: the supportive and smiling parent with her daughter.
- Faith: the ice-cream loving daughter waiting for her Dad to come home.
- Narrator: Symbolism Host

(ice-cream prop needed)

Setting:

A home kitchen area with dishes.

Begin Script

Faith:
(sits and eat ice-cream)

Wish me luck Mom. When Dad arrives home, I'm gonna ask him for a bigger allowance (Matthew 21:22).

Mother:
(cooks in the kitchen)

Good for you sweetie!

(pauses 2 seconds)

Do you think it might mean more chores for you to do?

Faith:
(looks up surprised)

I HOPE not!

(returns her focus to her ice-cream)

I don't want more work! But I'm sure when Dad senses my excitement (John 16:24), and sees my 'please face (Hebrews 11:6)', it will be all I need to make this happen (Mark 11:22)!

Mother:
I see…

(smiles to herself)

Well it's a good thing that doing the dishes is already a chore of yours (John 14:15)! Are you ready?

Faith:

Can I please finish my ice-cream first?

Mother:

(smiles)

Well... why don't you put it in the oven for later?

Faith:

But Mom... the oven is powered ON right now! My ice cream will turn to soup!

Mother:

(smiles at Faith and embraces her)

Always remember the lesson in this moment...

(pauses for 2 seconds)

Faith... without works is like ice cream in an oven. It's only one power-switch... away from having artificially warm feelings... which surely melt the 'Rocky Road' *before* you finish.

The End

Story Symbolism
- Faith = Confidence
- Ice Cream = Desire
- Oven = Warm Feeling
- Chores = Works
- Dishes = Obedience
- Allowance = Blessing
- Mom = Advisor
- Dad = Heavenly Father

Moral
A desire cannot be held too long inside initially warm feelings (John 2:14). Like ice cream in an oven, faith without works just melts away until 'solid' action is taken.

Share Your Thoughts
Is this parable your favorite?
Vote on our site!

Fun Facts
- The "Rocky Road" symbolizes both a flavor and a common pathway to a substantial blessing.
- Faith could see the "power-switch" on the oven, but not in herself.
- The dynamic of "daddy's little girl" represents the already pleasing dynamic between (actual) Faith and God (Hebrews 11:6).
- The Mom's smiles represent a natural version of a "warm feeling," rather than artificial development.
- "Ice cream" has a homonym effect with "I scream:" an emotional destiny to unfulfilled desires.

Discussion Questions

1. How do you feel about the "wish me luck" statement Faith began with? What about her reply "I hope not!" Use scripture to support your reaction?
2. Share a time in your life when you may have actually metaphorically "stored your ice cream in an oven." What "extra work" could you have added?
3. Share a 'rocky road' with your own faith in your life.

Instant Replay Bible Study

Scripture Index

Matthew 21:22
And whatever things you ask in prayer, believing, you will receive.
John 16:24
Until now you have asked nothing in My name. Ask, and you will receive, that your joy may be full.
Hebrews 11:6
But without faith it is impossible to please Him, for he who comes to God must believe that He is, and that He is a rewarder of those who diligently seek Him.
Mark 11:22
So Jesus answered and said to them, "Have faith in God.
John 14:15
"If you love Me, keep My commandments."

The
Family Skit
Version

Need More Scripts?
Become the bible lesson, rehearsing with family & friends through Kindle at a discount, and with less paper! Have fun.

The Parable of The Lawyer's Lullaby

A determined lawyer hires a Detective to solve a mystery around the courtroom conditions against her last case.

Characters

- Lawyer: the talented prosecutor, fixated on the mystery of unprofessional behavior in court.
- Detective: the agent with the firm called to investigate.
- Juror: the "surprise witness."
- Narrator: Presenter and Symbolism Host.

Props Needed: (a briefcase, a pen, and paper)

Setting

A law office and a separate court room within a courthouse.

<u>Begin Script</u>

Detective:
(stands outside the Lawyer's office door)

Lawyer:
(opens office door and motions and invite to the Detective inside)

Detective:
(head nods and quickly walks inside)

Narrator:
The Lawyer invites the firm's Detective into his office.

Lawyer:
I need your help.

(sits at desk)

Could you investigate the courtroom in my last trial? Something weird was going on in there!

Detective:
Sure. What happened?

Lawyer:
Well… every time I tried to cross-examine a witness… they became very sleepy, almost instantly!

Some even fell asleep on the stand! And the Judge just let them leave, one by one. It cheated me out of getting their testimony.

Detective:
Well... wait-a-second!

(pauses 2 seconds)

maybe *THAT* was the motive!

Without your evidence, this case would have to be dismissed, right? Are you sure the witnesses were really asleep? Maybe they were just PRETENDING to be asleep... for a creative escape (Isaiah 29:15).

Lawyer:
(knods head in agreement)

You know what? ... I was in the same courtroom and I was never sleepy!

Detective:
And you said the Judge simply excused them from the witness stand? Well... maybe the Judge was IN on this!

I mean... how else could this sleeping plan work?

Lawyer:
(stares at the Detective in awe)

Detective:
FORGET the courtroom conditions! We should investigate the Judge. What's his name?

(pulls out a pen and paper)

Lawyer:
It was…

(pauses 2 seconds)

…wow! I'm can't remember right now.

Detective:
No problem. What about the defendant's name? We can go from that?

Lawyer:
The defendant's name is….uhmm….

(pauses)

… is in my briefcase. Let me find it for you.

(looks around frantically for the briefcase as the Narrator continues)

Narrator:
The detective waits as the Lawyer scours his entire office.

Detective:
(motions to interrupt the Lawyer's search)

You know what…your case is so unique that I'm sure the courthouse can identify it and help me with the details.

I'll head over there now.

Lawyer:
Thank you Detective. I just know it's here somewhere. I'll call you with the information.

Detective:
(leaves the office and goes toward courtroom)

Narrator:
Arriving at the scene of the sleeping phenomenon, the Detective has the extra challenge of investigating without any names, case numbers, timeframes, or even a specific courtroom!

Detective:
(looks around the courthouse, recognizes something in the court room, and walks inside)

Narrator:
But before he can experience his full dilemma, the Detective sees the Lawyer's briefcase in a room which seems empty…

[SNORING]

Juror:
(appears sleeping and snoring in the courtroom)

Narrator:

…until he hears the sound of someone snoring. It is a female Juror fast asleep in the jury panel.

Detective:

(walks over slowly to awake the Juror as the Narrator continues)

Juror:

(slowly wakes up and looks at the Detective)

Narrator:

Stunned at her true sleep mode, the Detective knows there is more to discover. So he awakes the Juror.

Detective:

We should move you out this room. I wanna investigate what's causing everyone here to fall asleep.

Juror:

Oh…save your investigation! It was the Lawyer (Malachi 2:17).

Detective:

(appears surprised)

The lawyer?

Juror:

Yeah, it was the Lawyer's *lullaby* of a case!

(yawns)

Witness after witness took the stand. And no matter how honest, informative, or helpful their testimony was… the lawyer kept asking the same questions over and over again, like they never answered (Isaiah 42:20) (Proverbs 18:2)!

And the more exhausted the witness got, the more excited the lawyer became (Proverbs 14:8) until the Judge declared a mistrial (Proverbs 14:7). It was weird, pointless (Titus 3:9), and lot of other things! But the one thing it wasn't …was coffee.

Detective:
(walks around the court room like a lawyer)

I realize the trial is over. But I'm gonna cross-examine YOU now!

My lawyer friend complained about witnesses falling asleep BEFORE he got the chance to question, and not after like you describe. Can you explain that?

Juror:
Well that's not true. But I can still explain this… because, when I'm not a Juror, I'm a doctor. And based on the Lawyer's behavior, it's clear he has amnesia!

Detective:
(drops jaw but displays some doubt)

Juror:
I don't think the Lawyer even *remembers* how repetitive and ineffective she was being, or how rude she was to the

Judge (Proverbs 18:6). In fact, I'd be surprised if the Lawyer even remembered the Judge's name!

Detective:
(widens eyes more [John 9:39])

Juror:
I bet all this Lawyer remembers… are the mysterious conditions where he didn't get her way… and felt dismissed.

The End

Story Symbolism
- Lawyer (Prosecutor) = Reasoning
- Detective = Knowledge
- The Firm = Heart
- Courtroom = Conversation
- Witnesses = Clarity
- Sleepiness = Weariness (Spiritual Exhaustion)
- Briefcase = Bible
- Juror = Truth
- Case = Argument
- Judge = God Almighty
- Lawyer's Condition = Dismissive Behavior

Moral

Strife changes the Truth for itself. Peace changes itself for the Truth. Any "condition" that exhausts the process of knowledge itself can only be the beginning of a "cycle" of unproductive embarrassment and even more mystery. Don't be "a lawyer with amnesia." If we don't change our absence of mind, then we don't mind our absence of change.

Share Your Thoughts

Is this parable your favorite?
Vote on our site!

Fun Facts

- This entire court story never mentioned a defendant, only "something weird going on."
- Both Lawyer and Detective shared the same firm(ness), with initial reflexes toward each other (Proverbs 21:2).
- The Detective's discovery, without any real details, symbolizes the promise: seek and you shall find (Jeremiah 29:13).
- The case was officially declared a mistrial (temporary); it was not dismissed (final) (Matthew 3:2).

Discussion Questions

1. How would you rate the interrogation level of the Detective toward other characters?
2. What other reasons are possible for why the Detective was willing to begin an investigation with "an extra challenge" of no real details? Share a

similar story where determination skipped the details like the Detective.

3. How different would the story have been if the Detective were never called in?

Character Interaction

What kind of skills would a detective need to have to investigate without any details, like this one? Read the Detective's *Charity versus Ability* essay and "discover" 3 essential things to be effective in any "case!"

Instant Replay Bible Study

Scripture Index

Isaiah 29:15

Woe to those who seek deep to hide their counsel far from the LORD, and their works are in the dark. They say, "Who sees us?" and, "Who knows us?"

Malachi 2:17

You have wearied the LORD with your words. Yet you say, "In what way have we wearied Him?" In that you say, "Everyone who does evil Is good in the sight of the LORD, and He delights in them," or, "Where is the God of justice?"

Isaiah 42:20

Seeing many things, but you do not observe; opening the ears, but he does not hear.

Proverbs 18:2

A fool has no delight in understanding, but in expressing his own heart.

Proverbs 14:8

The wisdom of the prudent is to understand his way, but the folly of fools is deceit.

Proverbs 14:7
Go from the presence of a foolish man, when you do not perceive in him the lips of knowledge.

Titus 3:9
But avoid foolish disputes, genealogies, contentions, and strivings about the law; for they are unprofitable and useless.

Proverbs 18:6
A fool's lips enter into contention, and his mouth calls for blows.

John 9:39
And Jesus said, "For judgment I have come into this world, that those who do not see may see, and that those who see may be made blind."

The
Family Skit
Version

Need More Scripts?
Become the bible lesson, rehearsing with family & friends through Kindle at a discount, and with less paper! Have fun.

Peculiar Treasure (The Parable) (Poetry)

An 'enchanted wish' comes true in the 'closest' of ways!

Characters

- Poet & Narrator: the poet openly meditating on his enchanted wish for oneness with God
- Interacting Voice: the replying voice of God within the story poem to the poet
- Narrator (Optional): Symbolism Host

Setting

A general and poetic environment.

Begin Script

Poet:
(sits alone sharing openly with listeners)

No man exists with my enchanted wish
to craft a love affair with God and trust His management,
and graph above the stares I've gotten from abandonment
But yet, I couldn't understand it when HE granted this!
(II Corinthians 5:5) (Ephesians 1:13)

Imagine this: God said…

Interacting Voice:
…Enough repairs! You must be fair (Ephesians 4:30).
Prepare MY coming from upstairs
to interrupt these prayers.
From your heart, the truth is clever
But putting these clues together….
gives you your measure of 'peculiar treasure.'

I have merged your truth with pleasure many years ago.
I have blurred you views in pressure.
Any tear would know!
You empty fears should show exactly how,
so don't attack ME now…"

(walks slowly toward the poet)

Poet:
…then HE appeared in those attracting clouds (John 15:26).

With all my prayers that last for paragraphs,
I didn't dare to ask a thing except to spare the laugh
and share the facts
I said, "I'm ready for the clues you'll part with."
God replied…

Interacting Voice:
(motions pondering to himself)

How shall I start this
to prove your heart rich?

(looks directly at the poet)

I have evidence, Heaven sent, of your enchanted wish.
It has a puzzle-tested smile (Isaiah 11:2)
that's left your struggle less than mild (John 14:26).
The first to dance with
in your circumstances (Romans 8:9),
It's like a Couple blessed with child,
within one huddle-essence style (Galatians 5:22-23)!
Still guessing? It was my blessing to your urgent request.
And Mother Nature's still requesting a paternity test
(John 14:17).
'Cause who'd believe the Earth could surface this
(John 3:8)?
Somehow your birth certificate goes perfect with this wish.

But only hear It when you listen in (I Corinthians 2:13),
for a rest above words (Romans 8:26).
The Holy Spirit is my synonym
for 'Heaven on Earth (II Corinthians 3:17).'
So when I bless a fellow Christian

to digest My Melo System … (I Corinthians 6:19)
It proves your measure of peculiar treasure…. forever
(Romans 15:13).

The End

Poetry Symbolism
- Man = Christians
- Enchanted Wish = Oneness with God
- Peculiar Treasure = The Holy Spirit
- Upstairs = Heaven

Moral
No one can afford to overlook our current spiritual
shepherd: The Holy Spirit. Ever since Jesus rose again, our
Leader is so close to us… that It's inside us! And It's
influence is so overwhelming that even the world
acknowledges it through other nicknames (like
Conscience). So during our spiritual journey to the New
Testament's "Promised Land (Heaven)," in this wilderness
of a world, look no further for a sign. Look inside! God
Bless.

Share Your Thoughts
Is this parable your favorite?
Vote on our site!

Fun Facts
- The man was unknowingly interacting with and
  through his "enchanted wish" the entire time (John
  15:26)!

- Notice that God respected the man's request to "spare the laugh and share the facts."
- The "prayers that last for paragraphs" represent long, lengthy, traditional religious formats.
- Notice the easy-going, one-on-one dynamic the entire time.
- Realize that God actually did come down specifically to talk with the man about a better relationship.

Discussion Questions

1. When God jokingly said "don't attack ME now," what could HE have been making a subtle reference to?
2. Elaborate on the lyrics "…from your heart, the truth is clever."
3. What do you suppose God meant by saying, "Enough repairs?"
4. God respected the man's request to "spare the laugh and share the facts." How unique might this approach be compared to others with God?

Instant Replay Bible Study
Scripture Index

II Corinthians 5:5
Now He who has prepared us for this very thing is God, who also has given us the Spirit as a guarantee.
Ephesians 1:13
In Him you also trusted, after you heard the word of truth, the gospel of your salvation; in whom also, having believed, you were sealed with the Holy Spirit of promise.

Ephesians 4:30
And do not grieve the Holy Spirit of God, by whom you were sealed for the day of redemption.

John 15:26
But when the Helper comes, whom I shall send to you from the Father, the Spirit of truth who proceeds from the Father, He will testify of Me.

Isaiah 11:2
The Spirit of the LORD shall rest upon Him. The Spirit of wisdom and understanding, the Spirit of counsel and might, the Spirit of knowledge and of the fear of the LORD.

John 14:26
But the Helper, the Holy Spirit, whom the Father will send in My name, He will teach you all things, and bring to your remembrance all things that I said to you.

Romans 8:9
But you are not in the flesh but in the Spirit, if indeed the Spirit of God dwells in you. Now if anyone does not have the Spirit of Christ, he is not His.

Galatians 5:22-23
But the fruit of the Spirit is love, joy, peace, longsuffering, kindness, goodness, faithfulness, gentleness, self-control. Against such there is no law.

John 14:17
The Spirit of truth, whom the world cannot receive, because it neither sees Him nor knows Him; but you know Him, for He dwells with you and will be in you.

John 3:8
The wind blows where it wishes, and you hear the sound of it, but cannot tell where it comes from and where it goes. So is everyone who is born of the Spirit.

I Corinthians 2:13

These things we also speak, not in words which man's wisdom teaches but which the Holy Spirit teaches, comparing spiritual things with spiritual.

Romans 8:26

Likewise the Spirit also helps in our weaknesses. For we do not know what we should pray for as we ought, but the Spirit Himself makes intercession for us with groanings which cannot be uttered.

II Corinthians 3:17

Now the Lord is the Spirit; and where the Spirit of the Lord is, there is liberty.

I Corinthians 6:19

Or do you not know that your body is the temple of the Holy Spirit who is in you, whom you have from God, and you are not your own?

Romans 15:13

Now may the God of hope fill you with all joy and peace in believing, that you may abound in hope by the power of the Holy Spirit.

The
Family Skit
Version

Need More Scripts?
Become the bible lesson, rehearsing with family & friends through Kindle at a discount, and with less paper! Have fun.

Batteries Not Included (The Parable)

Jeffrey learns the difference between the game he is playing, and "the game he was playing!"

Characters

- Jeffrey: the video-game-loving kid salesman, with an abundant baseball card collection.
- Corey: the best friend of Jeffrey and reactor to a recent discovery.
- Narrator: Presenter and Symbolism Host.

Props Needed: (coins, baseball cards, video game player with a cord.)

Setting

In a living room with a pathway to a young boy's own room filled with batteries.

Begin Script

Corey:
(sits with Jeffrey in the living room, counts coins, and drops them into Jeffrey's hands)

Here you go.

Jeffrey:
Sold.

(collects the coins in his pocket)

I have more baseball cards for the same price.

Corey:
Wow. Even after all the one's you sold at school today, you still have some left? What are you saving up for anyway?

Jeffrey:
(motions Corey and walks to his room)

Come on… the cards are in my room.

Corey:
(follows Jeffrey inside)

Wow! You sure have a LOT of new batteries lying around in here! You should look for a way to sell these instead… to afford whatever you… what ARE you saving up for?

Jeffrey:
(motions a nervous pondering on how to answer)

Corey:
(begins to realize the answer)

Wait-a-minute. You sell your baseball cards… to buy all these batteries?

Jeffrey:
(appears embarrassed)

Yeah. But it's the only way to keep playing my video game! All these batteries are for my game player.

Corey:
Lemme see…

(picks up the game player)

Wait a second! This game player has a chord attached! Just plug it in, silly!

Jeffrey:
Corey, it's just too uncomfortable when it's plugged in (Exodus 20:18-19)! Who likes being tethered to the wall? I wanna feel further away and able to move around more (Exodus 20:21)!

Corey:

So... you're actually hoping to 'sell out' your birthday gift of baseball cards (I Corinthians 12:4), just to afford your plan to feel *LESS* connected (James 4:10)?

Sounds to me like a 'different game' with an 'extra controller (Matthew 6:24).'

Jeffrey:

(head nods and keeps listening as Corey continues)

Corey:

How far away and detached do you need to be inside the comfort of your own home? You're right beside an uninterrupted power source (Exodus 20:22), which your Father already paid for (I Corinthians 7:23) (John 3:16)! Keep the rest of your cards (Romans 12:6), keep the quality of your time and play. Stay connected (I Corinthians 12:27) (Exodus 20:20).

The End

Story Symbolism

- Home = God's Presence
- Baseball Cards = Gifts & Purpose
- Birthday Gift = Unique Gifts from God
- Sell = Trade (Sacrifice)
- Game Player = Heart
- Video Game = Lifestyle
- Power Source = God
- Batteries = Spiritual Distance
- Chord = Relationship with God

Moral

Direct fellowship with God will perfect the needs of a man's heart. But preferring more (cordless) distance begins a cycle of control and sacrifice of your God-given gifts until you have completely "sold out." Don't be your own Delilah and "cut yourself short." It's too costly for anyone. *"Start Over!"*

Share Your Thoughts

Is this parable your favorite?
Vote on our site!

Fun Facts

- The baseball cards symbolize the potential to discover extreme value.
- Jeff's character was inspired by Esau
- Jeff's full first name (Jeffrey) sounds "free."
- The moment where Jeff "ponders how to answer" symbolizes an unrehearsed public opinion.
- Corey's discovery of the chord did not surprise Tommy. He already realized it!

Discussion Questions

1. Despite realizing the chord before Chris, Tommy prefaced his dilemma by insisting the batteries were "the only way to get the playing time!" Was might his motivation had been?

Character Interaction

Take the *Stay Connected Challenge*
Continue to Chapter 4

Instant Replay Bible Study
Scripture Index

Exodus 20:18-19
Now all the people witnessed the thundering, the lightning flashes, the sound of the trumpet, and the mountain smoking; and when the people saw it, they trembled and stood afar off. Then they said to Moses, "You speak with us, and we will hear; but let not God speak with us…"
Exodus 20:21
So the people stood afar off, but Moses drew near the thick darkness where God was.
I Corinthians 12:4
There are diversities of gifts, but the same Spirit.
James 4:10
Humble yourselves in the sight of the Lord, and He will lift you up.
Matthew 6:24
No one can serve two masters; for either he will hate the one and love the other, or else he will be loyal to the one and despise the other. You cannot serve God and mammon.
Exodus 20:22
Then the LORD said to Moses, "Thus you shall say to the children of Israel: 'You have seen that I have talked with you from heaven.
I Corinthians 7:23
You were bought at a price; do not become slaves of men.
John 3:16
For God so loved the world that He gave His only begotten Son, that whoever believes in Him should not perish but have everlasting life.

Romans 12:6
Having then gifts differing according to the grace that is given to us, let us use them: if prophecy, let us prophesy in proportion to our faith;

I Corinthians 12:27
Now you are the body of Christ, and members individually.

Exodus 20:20
And Moses said to the people, "Do not fear; for God has come to test you, and that His fear may be before you, so that you may not sin."

Need More Scripts?
Become the bible lesson, rehearsing with family & friends through Kindle at a discount, and with less paper! Have fun.

The Parable of The Waitress's Tip

A mysteriously absent waitress adds insight to the menu for a starving customer.

Characters

- Waitress: the loveable and familiar customer service professional
- Eugene: a long time fellow customer of the restaurant with mysteriously increased hunger
- Narrator: Presenter and Symbolism Host

Props Needed: (platter: bread, fruits, a cup)

Setting

Inside a dining restaurant with a main table.

Begin Script

Eugene:
(walks inside, sits at main table, and holds his stomach)

Waitress:
(walks to Eugene's table)

Well HELLO again Eugene!

Eugene:
(smiles and looks up at the Waitress)

Waitress:
(hands Eugene a menu and pulls out a pad and pen)

What will it be today? Your usual lunch special?

Eugene:
Well that kinda depends, actually. Is it true that you guys are closing early today?

Waitress:
Yeah…we'll be closing early right before dinner time.

Eugene:
I see…

(hands the menu back without looking)

I'll have Combo One… Two… Three-Four-Five and Combo Six…with a Diet Cola please.

Waitress:
Well if your co-workers are all dining here, you could use our Banquet Room with a bigger table!

Eugene:
No… uhmm…this is all gonna be for me, just me.

Waitress:
(stares blankly at Eugene as he continues)

Eugene:
See I've been struggling with something inside me that just never feels full (John 16:24)! My appetite mysteriously just keeps on ticking to extra weight, but won't wait extra! So I'll need to eat Dinner for Lunch today too!

(looks down toward the table)

I apologize, I shouldn't bother you with my problems (Ecclesiastics 2:17).

Waitress:
That's okay! Let me bring you an appetizer immediately. I'll be right back!

(returns quickly with the 3-item platter)

Eugene:
Thank you, really!

(begins eating wildly)

Narrator:
Lots a time goes by with the Waitress nowhere in sight!

Eugene:
(looks frantically for the Waitress)

Narrator:
Finally Eugene sees her and gestures urgently.

Waitress:
(runs back to the table, looking around cautiously)

Eugene:
(smiles)

Listen, thanks so much for this appetizer so far. But whatever you guys haven't cooked yet, please don't!

(holds his stomach differently)

I can't explain why, but I feel great inside with no hunger after that miniature-sized appetizer! And of course I'll gladly pay for...

Waitress:
(interrupts)

We didn't make any of them.

(smiles)

I knew we wouldn't need too.

Eugene:
Really! How did you know?

Waitress:
Well… I only work here to put myself through college to become a Nutritionist. So I am educated on the natural way digestion works!

The platter I gave you is organic (John 6:35) (Galatians 5:22-23) (Psalms 23:5): free from the artificial preservatives designed to keep people hungry.

Eugene:
Are you serious? There are ingredients like that?

Waitress:
Oh yeah!

(sits down with Eugene and speaks lower)

There are chemicals to make bread rise more attractively (Luke 12:1), and artificial sweeteners to change energy levels (I Timothy 5:13).

And unfortunately Eugene, I'm dishing about the dishes here! I just found out today that this place uses them.

Eugene:
So *THIS* is the reason for my appetite.

Waitress:

It's also the reason for this place closing early. The Chef quit... right after I did this morning (Psalms 1:1)! In fact, I'm not even supposed to be here right now! But I've been hiding around so I can warn my favorite customers.

Eugene:

I can't thank you enough! Can I pay you for the appetizer?

Waitress:

It's on me (I Thessalonians 5:14) (Isaiah 49:4)

(leans in closer)

Eugene you're a great and generous customer. So let *me* give *YOU* a tip this time.

Since this is the only restaurant in town, start growing your own healthy foods (Proverbs 12:11), and learn how to cook (Psalms 128:2) (II Timothy 2:15). The appetite you once had is nothing compared to the appetite of this business. It's like a "bottomless pit (Proverbs 30:16)!

The End

Story Symbolism
- Restaurant = Earth
- Appetite = Purpose
- Hunger = Void in the Heart
- Organic = Natural Intent
- Waitress = Truth
- Eugene = Mankind
- Chef = Compromise
- Artificial Ingredients = Man-made Influence
- Cooking = Bible Study
- Bread Chemical = Leaven of the Pharisees
- Menu = Earthly Satisfaction
- Artificial Sweeteners = Vain Motivation
- Appetizer = Bread of Life & Fruits of Holy Spirit

Moral
There's no appetite to sin around the spiritual "bread" of life, "fruits" of the Holy Spirit, and a "cup" that runneth over! Avoid the "aftertaste" of vanity. And always remember that nothing "serves" a man better than the truth. God bless!

Share Your Thoughts
Is this parable your favorite?
Vote on our site!

Fun Facts
- Realize the quitting order: first the Waitress (Truth), then the Chef (Compromise).
- Eugene's order, without looking at the menu, symbolizes that he's "seen it all before."

- The news about the restaurant's early closing probably came from "a sign."
- Notice the Waitress reflex to "sit down and whisper with" Eugene, when he pursued more knowledge.

Discussion Questions

1. Overall how would you rate the Waitress's customer service skills?
2. Why do you think the Waitress responded to Eugene's needs first, before offer the bigger picture?
3. How do you feel about the Waitress hiding around after quitting to warn her favorite customers?
4. Notice how "that's okay" was the Waitress's reply, when Eugene felt he share too much on his personal challenges to her. How beneficial was this?

Character Interaction

She's ready to 'dish about those dishes!' After all, the Waitress no longer works for them anymore, right? As she continues hiding around to warn more customers, you have a unique opportunity to help her spread this fulfilling message further! Read and share her rhyming mission as a *Camouflaged Prophet* in Chapter 4. God bless!

Instant Replay Bible Study

Scripture Index

John 16:24

Until now you have asked nothing in My name. Ask, and you will receive, that your joy may be full.

Ecclesiastics 2:17
Therefore I hated life because the work that was done under the sun was distressing to me, for all is vanity and grasping for the wind.

John 6:35
And Jesus said to them, "I am the bread of life. He who comes to Me shall never hunger, and he who believes in Me shall never thirst.

Galatians 5:22-23
But the fruit of the Spirit is love, joy, peace, longsuffering, kindness, goodness, faithfulness, gentleness, self-control. Against such there is no law.

Psalms 23:5
You prepare a table before me in the presence of my enemies. You anoint my head with oil; my cup runs over.

Luke 12:1
In the meantime, when an innumerable multitude of people had gathered together, so that they trampled one another, He began to say to His disciples first of all, "Beware of the leaven of the Pharisees, which is hypocrisy."

I Timothy 5:13
And besides they learn to be idle, wandering about from house to house, and not only idle but also gossips and busybodies, saying things which they ought not.

Psalms 1:1
Blessed is the man who walks not in the counsel of the ungodly, nor stands in the path of sinners, nor sits in the seat of the scornful.

I Thessalonians 5:14
Now we exhort you, brethren, warn those who are unruly, comfort the fainthearted, uphold the weak, be patient with all.

Isaiah 49:4

Then I said, 'I have labored in vain, I have spent my strength for nothing and in vain. Yet surely my just reward is with the LORD. And my work with my God.'"

Proverbs 12:11

He who tills his land will be satisfied with bread. But he who follows frivolity is devoid of understanding.

Psalms 128:2

When you eat the labor of your hands, you shall be happy, and it shall be well with you.

II Timothy 2:15

Be diligent to present yourself approved to God, a worker who does not need to be ashamed, rightly dividing the word of truth.

Proverbs 30:16

Sheol, the barren womb, the earth that is not satisfied with water. And the fire never says, "Enough!"

The
Family Skit
Version

Need More Scripts?
Become the bible lesson, rehearsing with family & friends through Kindle at a discount, and with less paper! Have fun.

The Parable of The Counselor's Gift

A school counselor gains exaggerated popularity amongst a curious news reporter, despite a statistical mystery.

Characters

- News Reporter: the skeptical investigative journalist called to interview the Counselor.
- Counselor: the school's most popular most admired official (who requested the interview).
- Cameraman: supporting co-worker always at the side of the News Reporter.
- Secretary: supporting co-worker to the Counselor.
- School Boy 1: schoolboy at the center of media attention.
- Extras: School fans of the Counselor
- Extras: Security Guards
- Narrator: Presenter and Symbolism Host.

Props Needed: (microphone, video camera, tape recorder)

Setting:

In an interview newsroom with a separate school grounds principals office, showing a Door 1 and Door 2

Begin Script

Counselor:
(sits at the table with the News Reporter and smiles)

It's a gift! It's…it's a gift!

(continues smiling as the Narrator continues)

Narrator:
The School Counselor explains this to the news reporter… again! And it seems to be her answer to every question, even though SHE asked for this interview. "It's a gift" is all she offers to explain her sudden popularity.

Surveys score this School Counselor at number one: more admired than the Principal (II Timothy 2:10), the Coach (II Corinthians 1:6), and all the teachers combined (Galatians 3:24)! The news reporter continues trying for a variety of answers.

News Reporter:
(holds his tape recorder close)

Well what about the scoring pattern, Counselor? I notice you score highest with kids involved in school fights. Could you talk specifically about how you inspire them? How do you do it?

Counselor:
(motions talking silently as Narrator continues)

Narrator:

The School Counselor does open up more. But her responses seem very basic with nothing unique enough to justify her isolated success. From "let you smile be your umbrella" to "forget your troubles and just get happy," the journalist sits both confused and unimpressed (Luke 18:7). His next question probes deeper.

News Reporter:

And despite 'the gift' you have, Counselor, school fights have actually been on the rise (Proverbs 29:9)!

Now it's actually been suggested that some kids are literally fighting to see you. Some believe their misbehavior is only done to skip the long waiting line to make an appointment with you, Counselor! How do you respond? Or maybe you have a different theory to helps us understand.

Counselor:

Well I think that maybe it's a challenge for me to be even less selfish... with my gift!

News Reporter:

(appears frustrated)

I see.

(stops his tape recorder)

Well... would it be okay, Counselor, to see you in action one day?

P a g e **177**

Counselor:
I'll share my gift, sure!

News Reporter & Counselor:
(shake each other's hand and leave the interview table)

Narrator:
The next day… another school fight occurs (Proverbs 29:10).

The one-sided battle between an Honor student and his bully increases the crowd and the chaos longer than usual (Proverbs 17:12). So the Counselor is desperately called. Live news cameras follow behind them as they walk into the Principals Office.

Cameraman:
(walks with News Reporter to the Counselor's and shakes her hand)

Counselor, News Reporter, and Cameraman:
(walk together inside the school)

Counselor:
(approaches the Secretary at her desk)

Okay… where are the boys?

Secretary:
We separated them. Bully is Room 1. Honor student… Room 2.

Counselor:
Thanks.

(turns around to the News Reporter)

Okay I always deal with the more likely victim first which is the Honor student in Room 2. I'll speak to him alone.

News Reporter:
Absolutely!

Cameraman:
(stands behind News Reporter and head nods)

Narrator:
As the Counselor heads inside, her school fans eavesdrop next to the door for the magical conversation they expect.

School Extras:
(lean on the door motioning listening)

Narrator:
But the only words they can make out are the same phrases they use: "let your smile be your umbrella," and "forget your troubles and just get happy!"

Five minutes pass, the door re-opens, and an instantly overjoyed schoolboy walks out.

School Boy 1:
(walks out the room smiling and happy)

School Extras:
(echoes to each other)

Amazing…it truly is a gift!

School Boy 1:
(tugs the Counselor's hand)

Narrator:
The little boy is now even trying to make arraignments to talk with the other boy.

News Reporter:
That's so mature of you young man. But I think the Counselor is first!

Counselor:
Actually…the security guards are first!

Security Guard Extras:
(arrive preparing to go inside Room 2)

Counselor:
It's our school policy to always send them in first to determine if the bigger aggressor is calm enough and I'm safe enough to go in.

News Reporter:
Sure!

Security Guards:
(go in and quickly return shaking their heads against it)

Counselor:
(head nods back)

Well it looks like I'm done here. We'll all just need to be more patient with the other boy.

School Boy 1:
Sure!

(gives the Counselor a hug)

Cameraman:
(films the hug)

Incredible!

Counselor:
(turns to the News Reporter)

Thank you for coming.

(whispers into his ear and leaves)

Narrator:
Pulling him closer, the Counselor whispers in his ear, "I told you… it's a gift."

[APPLAUSE]

Applause surrounds the Principals office as she leaves smiling. But still curious about the increase in school fights, the reporter asks to interview the other boy (I Thessalonians 5:9).

Security Guards:
(some block the door, while others motions for the News Reporter to leave)

Narrator:
Immediately the guards fiercely block the door (Matthew 23:13). But even quicker are other school officials insisting the entire news team leave. And suddenly the mystery becomes clear to him.

News Reporter:
Oh my…

(runs in the other direction past everyone)

I think we have an even bigger story.

Cameraman:
(follows the News Reporter confused)

Extras:
(follow motioning curiosity with each other)

Narrator:
Rushing to the secretary, the reporter stares in disbelief.

News Reporter:
You switched the boys and the rooms!

Secretary:
(appears shocked but motionless)

Narrator:
The secretary shivers as the crowd develops.

News Reporter:
You tricked the Counselor into consoling the bully, and ignoring the real victim (Ecclesiastics 9:16)! And you used the security guards to block off the right entrance (Psalms 94:21)!

Security Guards:
(immediately push others out the way to leave as the Narrator continues)

Narrator:
The security guards rush to the exit with their guilt, pushing news cameras away.

Cameraman:
So the REAL reason fights keep happening here is because the School Counselor bullies the guilt these bullies have developed from their own bullying until it disappears (Proverbs 17:15)!

School Extras:
(gather and stare as the News Reporter continues [Proverbs 18:5)])

News Reporter:
It's *NOT* a gift! It's a deception that you're causing the Counselor and everyone else to believe (Proverbs 24:24)! Oh, you are in big trouble (Isaiah 5:20). Someone get me to The Principal!

Secretary:
Good luck with that. You won't believe this either … but I was just doing my job! And I don't work for HIM. I work for *her*.
The End

Story Symbolism
- School Counselor = Simplicity
- Secretary (Assistant): Manipulation
- News Reporter = Righteousness (Hunger and Thirst)
- School Fights = Strife
- Cameraman = Public Viewpoint
- Survey = Opinions
- The Principal = The Principle of Righteousness
- Teacher - Official Advisors
- School = The World
- Interview - Testing the Spirits
- Gift = Presents (of Presence)
- Honor Student = Wisdom
- Bully = Folly
- Security Guards = Advice
- School Policy = Tradition

Moral

Simplicity is willing to manipulate itself and betray wisdom just to be popular (believe it or not). So its mysterious 'gift' that merely sounds like presents (presence) should be fairly questioned (or interviewed). Simplicity is a lukewarm intervention more likely to protect vanity, and block truth. Any authority lacking a real "hunger and thirst for righteousness" will only increase the ongoing struggle between wisdom and folly.

Share Your Thoughts

Is this parable your favorite?
Vote on our site!

Fun Facts

- It was the Counselor who asked for the interview, not the other way around (Proverbs 16:19).
- The Counselor's private whisper animates a reprobate mind (Romans 1:28).
- The (non-questionable) school policy (tradition) was the only thing the Counselor was specific about.
- The eavesdropping fans could not make out any questions (just rhetorical statements).

Discussion Questions

1. Interpret the very last line in the story: "I don't work for HIM, I work for her."
2. What do you think the other boy would have told the news reporter (in scripture)?
3. Imagine how the Counselor's fans felt around the news crew? Explain why.

Character Interaction

No one got the other side, hearing from the other boy: the real Honor Student. But you can! Read his essay *The Top 20 Biblical Signs of a Fool*

Instant Replay Bible Study

Scripture Index

Galatians 3:24
Therefore the law was our tutor to bring us to Christ, that we might be justified by faith.
II Timothy 2:10
Therefore I endure all things for the sake of the elect, that they also may obtain the salvation which is in Christ Jesus with eternal glory.
II Corinthians 1:6
Now if we are afflicted, it is for your consolation and salvation, which is effective for enduring the same sufferings which we also suffer. Or if we are comforted, it is for your consolation and salvation.
Luke 18:7
And shall God not avenge His own elect who cry out day and night to Him, though He bears long with them?
Proverbs 29:9
If a wise man contends with a foolish man, whether the fool rages or laughs, there is no peace
Proverbs 29:10
The bloodthirsty hate the blameless. But the upright seek his well-being.
Proverbs 17:12
Let a man meet a bear robbed of her cubs, rather than a fool in his folly.

I Thessalonians 5:9
For God did not appoint us to wrath, but to obtain salvation through our Lord Jesus Christ.

Matthew 23:13
But woe to you, scribes and Pharisees, hypocrites! For you shut up the kingdom of heaven against men; for you neither go in yourselves, nor do you allow those who are entering to go in.

Ecclesiastics 9:16
Wisdom is better than strength. Nevertheless the poor man's wisdom is despised. And his words are not heard.

Psalms 94:21
They gather together against the life of the righteous, and condemn innocent blood.

Proverbs 17:15
He who justifies the wicked, and he who condemns the just, both of them alike are an abomination to the LORD.

Proverbs 18:5
It is not good to show partiality to the wicked, Or to overthrow the righteous in judgment.

Proverbs 24:24
He who says to the wicked, "You are righteous," him the people will curse; Nations will abhor him.

Isaiah 5:20
Woe to those who call evil good, and good evil; who put darkness for light, and light for darkness; who put bitter for sweet, and sweet for bitter!

The
Family Skit
Version

Need More Scripts?
Become the bible lesson, rehearsing with family & friends through Kindle at a discount, and with less paper! Have fun.

The Parable of the Calendar's Watch

A "familiar" celebrity is asked to help promote a mysterious product.

Characters

- The Celebrity: the hugely popular female talent arriving to sign autographs.
- Mr. Calendar: the business promoter and calendar salesman.
- The Gentleman: the inspiring character eager to meet the celebrity.
- The Agent: a networker to the Celebrity who acts surprisingly out of character.
- Extras: Extremely animated fans of the Celebrity.
- 2 Group Extras: the bodyguards for the Celebrity
- Narrator: Presenter and Symbolism Host.

Props Needed: (many calendar visuals, a cross, a pen)

Setting

The inside of a large store, followed by the inside of an upscale restaurant.

Begin Script

Everyone (except the Celebrity & Bodyguards):
(stand silently and stare at the main door)

Celebrity & Bodygaurds:
(slowly walk inside the store)

Everyone (except Celebrity & Bodyguards):

[APPLAUSE & CHEERS]

(stand up jumping routinely)

Celebrity:
(smiles and waves to fans)

[APPLAUSE & CHEERS]

Narrator:
The cheers get louder and louder as the Celebrity walks inside the store.

Celebrity:
(walks toward Mr. Calendar and shakes his hand)

Narrator:
She shakes the business promoter's hand and then waves hers to the cheering crowd: each one with a calendar in their hand.

Everyone:
(waves their calendar visual in the air continuously as the Narrator continues)

Narrator:
Simply buying this store's calendar today earns them an autograph and chance to meet the star in person! And with her fan club of jumping girls and blushing boys, this store has already sold out (I Peter 4:8). So the promoter rushes out to make more copies.

Celebrity:
(walks around interacting with all her fans as the Narrator continues)

Narrator:
Meanwhile, the cheers follow the Celebrity as she meets, poses for pictures, and finally signs everyone's calendar.

Celebrity:
(looks up, sees the Gentleman, and pauses)

Narrator:
But in the corner of her eye, she sees a separate stand with a gentleman selling another product. Whatever it is doesn't appear to be doing nearly as well as the calendars (I Corinthians 13:4).

Mr. Calendar:
(runs back and returns with many more calendars)

So… mark your calendars folks. Because she, and our wonderful calendars, will be returning back here soon!

Everyone:
[APPLAUSE]

Narrator:
Applause erupts again as the event planners thank her.

Everyone:
(follow after the celebrity while cheering)

Agent:
(joins the Celebrity's side and motions being on an important a cell phone call)

Bodyguards:
(gather around the Celebrity)

Narrator:
And as the chasing crowd moves to the left, she gets a much clearer view of the gentleman salesman. Still trying to make out exactly what product he's selling, she leaves for lunch.

Celebrity:
(exits with the bodyguards)

[SCENE 2]

Celebrity & Agent:
(sits at the table inside the restaurant)

Agent:
(continues motioning an important cell phone call)

Narrator:
Now inside the restaurant with her agent, the Celebrity notices the people in her VIP section disappear, running toward a new arriving guest.

Celebrity:
(looks up at that direction)

Gentleman:
(walks inside very humble)

Narrator:
And the Celebrity realizes it's the same less popular gentleman vendor at the marketplace event.

Gentleman:
(passes out an [hands only] unseen product to random people as the Narrator continues)

Extras:
(smile with gratitude as the Narrator continues)

Agent:
(quickly leaves table without excusing himself)

Narrator:
The older gentleman hands out the same mysterious product to all who simply ask. The Celebrity also realizes

that even her agent has also left their table to shake the gentleman's hand (Isaiah 29:19).

Celebrity:
(stares at the Gentleman)

Narrator:
"Just who is this guy?" the Celebrity wonders, "and what is he selling?"

Gentleman:
(smiles and whispers into the Agent's ear)

Narrator:
The gentleman smiles at her stare and whispers an equally mysterious request in her agent's ear.

Agent:
(drops his phone, takes the Gentleman's hand, and walks back to the table as the Narrator continues)

Narrator:
Her agent excitedly takes his hand and walks the gentleman to the Celebrity's table.

Gentleman:
I'm a huge fan of you!

Celebrity:
I really appreciate it!

(picks up a pen, looks for his calendar to sign, but can't see it)

Thank you sir!

(pulls out her own sample Calendar to sign but is interrupted)

Gentleman:
I was just talking with your agent, hoping you would consider endorsing my product instead of Mr. Calendar's (Romans 11:14).

Agent:
(interrupts excitedly)

Oh ... we *ACCEPT* (I Peter 1:22)!

Celebrity:
Well... *(laughs)* wait-a-second... I would like to know more if I may!

Gentleman:
(smiles)

Of course (Matthew 11:29)!

Celebrity:
Please have a seat, sir!

Agent:
Here take my chair, Sir!

(pulls it out like a waiter)

You guys discuss the details while I'll find our waiter for another chair!

(leaves)

Extras:
(point to Celebrity's table, whisper to each other, and give a thumbs up to the Celebrity)

Gentleman:
(begins to sit down as the narrator continues)

Narrator:
As the gentleman sits down next to her, customers peek with smiles and thumbs up, cheering on the lucky one. It is unclear to the Celebrity which one she is. The gentleman begins.

Gentleman:
I know what Mr. Calendar has agreed to pay you. But I am prepared to offer you even more.

Celebrity:
Well … with all due respect, sir, your product didn't seem as popular at the store event.

Gentleman:
(smiles)

You can't always believe what you see (John 9:39).

I own the entire marketplace! Mr. Calendar rented today's limited time here. I was just keeping an eye on my store (Job 1:7).

Celebrity:
(head nods and leans in more as he continues)

Gentleman:
Today's shoppers only see the decorations of a crafty businessman (II Corinthians 4:4): celebrity appeal, commercials, and a chance to party with the majority for a price. But the big picture has Mr. Calendar in huge debt (Romans 6:23). He secretly needs your endorsement for access to your fans, which means a chance to sell items and be less 'in the red (Revelation 12:12).'

Celebrity:
Well… how can Mr. Calendar afford me then?

Gentleman:
He can't! Mr. Calendar put tricks in your contract to avoid paying you.

Narrator:
The Celebrity's begins to remember her contract's complicated language (II Corinthians 2:11).

Gentleman:
But his business tactics go even further (I Peter 5:8)!

(points to Celebrity's sample calendar)

Look closer at his calendar that everyone bought today. Do you see anything odd about it?

Celebrity:
(stares at the calendar for 2 seconds)

Oh my goodness! It's LAST year's calendar!

(pause 2 more seconds)

Gentleman:
That's right. Mr. Calendar is all about the money even when it means deliberately selling items that are worthless and outdated with no real value (Isaiah 3:9). He uses your fans' appetite to meet you as camouflage.

Celebrity:
(widens her eyes)

We've got to DO something! Some people are living according to that outdated material.

Gentleman:
(head nods in agreement)

For all his offenses, I will to drive him out soon. But right now I am more concerned about the unsuspecting customers (Romans 11:15).

Celebrity:

Well if it's your business, what are you waiting for, sir? You could do it right now!

Gentleman:

For the customers' sake, the real competition is between his craftiness and my truth. And this is exactly the message I would like to share while endorsing my free product. Mr. Calendar won't be able to compete.

Celebrity:

Why… is your product a calendar too?

Gentleman:

My product is SO much better than a calendar (James 5:20) (I Peter 4:7)!

Celebrity:

So let me get this straight. You want to hire me for a celebrity endorsement of your free product: a product that you believe will somehow put Mr. Calendar out of business because, in your opinion, your product is BETTER than a calendar! What IS this product you created?

Gentleman:

(reaches in his pocket, pulls out a cross)

It's called eternal life!

The End

Moral

Sin is about as cheap and outdated as a *Clearance Sale* on last year's calendar. Buy Eternal Life, freely given by God's grace. The children of God are like anointed celebrities appealing to the heart of man. The real celebration is salvation. Start spreading the news!

Share Your Thoughts

Is this parable your favorite?
Vote on our site!

Story Symbolism

- The Celebrity = *You!*
- The Gentleman = God
- Agent = Heart
- Crowd = Mankind
- Fans = Family and Friends (of You)
- Event = Life
- Calendar = Sin (For a Season)
- Store = Earth
- Restaurant = Spiritual Realm
- Endorse = Live For
- Autograph = Proclaim
- Mr. Calendar = Satan
- Payment = Blessing
- Contract = Supernatural Intentions
- Restaurant Staff = Angels
- Rented Time = Earthy Time for a Season

Fun Facts

- No one ate at the table while the gentleman spoke, unless you count "HIS every word (Mathew 4:4)."
- The Celebrity first view of the gentleman at the store was from the "right" angle.
- The agent (heart) demonstrated the same fan club setting for the Gentlemen (God).
- The excitement of the agent (heart) caused behavior out of traditional character, as it should.
- The whisper into the agent's ear represents the privacy between God's voice and his children.
- The gentleman's "smile at her stares" represents the God's reaction to anyone seeking his face.
- Notice the gentleman never actually had a calendar himself (pure, without sin).
- The gentleman referred to their setting as "my" restaurant, in addition to the marketplace he owns.
- The owner was against a full monopoly.
- The gentleman being patient with his intervention was ultimately to protect the naïve customers from the effect of a riot.
- The gentleman adjusted himself to the Celebrity's auditioning norms before showing her the big picture.
- Not one episode of envy centered around the restaurant.
- The customers at the restaurant symbolize "new creatures" being served (still competing to serve God).
- The gentleman beginning statement, "I'm a huge fan of you," animated how God loved us first.

- The gentleman did not speak competitively; he only spoke truthfully.

Discussion Questions

1. When has your own "agent (heart)" been moved toward the gentleman (God) almost independently out of natural excitement, like in the story? Share this moment.
2. If The Gentleman claimed his success was self-made by his "blood, sweat, and tears," which scripture(s) supports this.
3. How do you feel about the gentleman's stating "the real competition is between his craftiness and my truth?"

Character Interaction

The story never mentioned actually was The Celebrity is famous *for*! She is a musical communicator (Rapper). But now, with her new endorsement deal, she is a new and improved Christian Rapper. Experience her uplifting lyrics in Perception Bearer in Chapter 4. Have fun!

Instant Replay Bible Study

Scripture Index

I Peter 4:8
And above all things have fervent love for one another, for "love will cover a multitude of sins.
I Corinthians 13:4
Love suffers long and is kind; love does not envy; love does not parade itself, is not puffed up.

Isaiah 29:19
The humble also shall increase their joy in the LORD, and the poor among men shall rejoice in the Holy One of Israel.

Romans 11:14
If by any means I may provoke to jealousy those who are my flesh and save some of them.

I Peter 1:22
Since you have purified your souls in obeying the truth through the Spirit in sincere love of the brethren, love one another fervently with a pure heart.

Matthew 11:29
Take My yoke upon you and learn from Me, for I am gentle and lowly in heart, and you will find rest for your souls.

John 9:39
And Jesus said, "For judgment I have come into this world, that those who do not see may see, and that those who see may be made blind."

Job 1:7
And the LORD said to Satan, "From where do you come?" So Satan answered the LORD and said, "From going to and fro on the earth, and from walking back and forth on it."

II Corinthians 4:4
Whose minds the god of this age has blinded, who do not believe, lest the light of the gospel of the glory of Christ, who is the image of God, should shine on them.

Romans 6:23
For the wages of sin is death, but the gift of God is eternal life in Christ Jesus our Lord.

Revelation 12:12
Therefore rejoice, O heavens, and you who dwell in them! Woe to the inhabitants of the earth and the sea! For the devil has come down to you, having great wrath, because he knows that he has a short time."

II Corinthians 2:11

Lest Satan should take advantage of us; for we are not ignorant of his devices.

I Peter 5:8

Be sober, be vigilant; because your adversary the devil walks about like a roaring lion, seeking whom he may devour.

Isaiah 3:9

The look on their countenance witnesses against them, and they declare their sin as Sodom. They do not hide it. Woe to their soul! For they have brought evil upon themselves.

Romans 11:15

For if their being cast away is the reconciling of the world, what will their acceptance be but life from the dead?

James 5:20

Let him know that he who turns a sinner from the error of his way will save a soul from death and cover a multitude of sins.

I Peter 4:7

But the end of all things is at hand; therefore be serious and watchful in your prayers.

The
Family Skit
Version

Need More Scripts?
Become the bible lesson, rehearsing with family & friends through Kindle at a discount, and with less paper! Have fun.

The Parable of The Blindfold
A patient sneaks to another doctor for a second opinion.

Characters
- Thomas: the health-seeking desert dweller in the midst of competing philosophies.
- Lady Luck: the aggressive and controversial doctor of the dessert with Thomas as a patient (debuts in Part 2)
- Secretary: the clerical professional awaiting Thomas.
- Doctor Powers: the new, more distant, and highly recommended doctor sought after by Thomas.
- Narrator: Presenter and Symbolism Host.

Props Needed: (telephone, map, business card, doctor's note, picture, and car visual)

Setting:
A home bedroom. Later a separate doctor's clinic and office.

Begin Script

Thomas:
(sits on his bed and holds a telephone to his ear)

Narrator:
Thomas tilts with his telephone in the early morning, preparing to leave a message.

Thomas:
Yes hello… I'm a patient at The Lucky Ones Clinic. And I need to cancel my appointment today with my doctor, Lady Luck. Something came up (Psalms 118:8). But I have enough of your *4-Leaf-Clover* cream to last me until we can reschedule. Thanks! Bye.

(drops phone, picks up the map, and stares at it)

Narrator:
Thomas drops the phone next to a map he is still starring at, along with a business card he kept (Proverbs 3:5), matching the addresses (Proverbs 3:6).

Thomas:
(leaves to his car as the Narrator continues)

Narrator:
And practically tip-toeing to his car, Thomas proceeds out of town to the new destination.

Thomas:
(arrives and walks inside the Doctor's office)

Secretary:
(sits at her desk smiling at Thomas)

Hi… can I help you sir?

Thomas:
Good morning! I'm Thomas Walker and have an appointment with Doctor Powers.

Secretary:
Sure! Please follow me to the office.

(leads Thomas to the doctor's office)

Thomas:
(walks with the secretary and looks around cautiously)

Narrator:
Thomas continues to look around ensuring he's not noticed by anyone from his town.

Doctor Powers:
(walks inside the doctor's office)

Good morning…is it Thomas Walker?

Thomas:
Oh, Dr. Powers…

(shakes her hand)

Thanks for agreeing see me.

Doctor Powers:
My pleasure (II Corinthians 1:24). But we're on a first name basis here. Please just call me Faith.

Thomas:
You got it! Well Faith… I heard about you through my friend Christian. She tells me you're the best!

Doctor Powers:
Well… *(pauses 2 seconds)* it's actually a team effort. Let's make it YOUR turn to feel better! How can I help?

Thomas:
Well my skin type is extremely sensitive to sunlight. And I live in a desert, with no real way to block it! Until I can afford to move, I've been using a medicated *4-Leaf-Clover Cream* to lessen the effects.

(shows her a cream bottle)

Dr. Powers:
(examines the bottle)

Wow…someone must have to really 'lay it on thick!

Thomas:
Yeah, my original doctor does. It helps a little, but it's really expensive! And she insists it's the only way! So I guess I'm here for a second opinion.

Doctor Powers:
Sure. Let's run some tests and I think I can help you with that.

(motions checking Thomas arm like checking for blood pressure)

Narrator:
Much to the surprise of Thomas, Faith actually begins by checking his blood pressure.

Doctor Powers:
Oh this is good news!

(motions checking levels on a screen)

Thomas I'm happy to offer you a cheaper and better alternative. Based on these tests, your condition actually needs *physical* therapy, not medicated creams. And, if you like, we can begin right now!

Thomas:
Absolutely!

Doctor Powers:
So let's head to my operating room. And, for this to work, I'll need to blindfold you first (Hebrews 11:1). Then I'll

take your hand and lead you inside a machine where you'll vary your speeds when I tell you to. Are you ready?

Narrator:
Although unsure how this will help, Thomas submits. And Faith begins her unique procedure.

[END OF SCENE]

[SCENE 2]

Thomas:
(slowly wakes up in his bedroom)

Narrator:
Time passes by unnoticed as Thomas awakes from a deep sleep. And he finds himself somehow back inside his bed at home!

Thomas:
(discovers a note on his bed, picks it up as Narrator continues)

Narrator:
But before he can call this whole experience a dream, he notices a doctor's note signed by Faith (Romans 10:17). But as he holds it up to the window to read it, no sunlight shines through. In fact there's no heat to be felt either!

Thomas:
(gets up, turns on a lamp, and stares at his skin surprised as the Narrator continues)

Narrator:
Puzzled, Thomas turns on a lamp. And he immediately notices his incredibly smooth, cooled, healthy skin.

Thomas:
Oh my!

(unknowingly drops the letter, runs to mirror, and stares inside)

Narrator:
Thomas drops the letter and runs to his mirror. He looks completely revitalized and renewed. But along with his image reflection, he sees a new, giant object outside his window.

Thomas:
(turns around quickly and puts his hand over his own mouth)

Narrator:
Turning around, Thomas finally realizes what has happened: somehow a mountain has *moved* to block the sunlight from the house, forever protecting his skin condition (II Timothy 4:7).

Thomas:
(jumping and cheering)

Narrator:
After hours of pinching himself and crying tears of joy, Thomas returns to Faith's note.

Thomas:
(picks the doctor's not up again to read it)

Narrator:
It reads: 'Keep the rest of these mustard seeds, Thomas.
Doctor's orders!'
To Be Continued

*Stand firm with Faith as this parable continues and Faith
is tested!

Story Symbolism
- Lady Luck = Superstitions, Myths
- Dr. Faith Powers = Faith
- (Doubting) Thomas = Mankind
- Business Card = Change
- Map = Mind State
- Prescriptions = Insistence
- Desert = Deserted Place
- Christian = Fellowship
- Skin = Potential
- Sunlight = Exposure to Doubt
- Physical Therapy = Action

Moral, Discussion Questions, & Fun Facts revealed after
full story*

Instant Replay Bible Study
Scripture Index

Psalms 118:8
It is better to trust in the LORD than to put confidence in man.

Proverbs 3:5
Trust in the LORD with all your heart, and lean not on your own understanding.

Proverbs 3:6
In all your ways acknowledge Him, and He shall direct your paths.

II Corinthians 1:24
Not that we have dominion over your faith, but are fellow workers for your joy; for by faith you stand.

Hebrews 11:1
Now faith is the substance of things hoped for, the evidence of things not seen.

Romans 10:17
So then faith comes by hearing, and hearing by the word of God.

II Timothy 4:7
I have fought the good fight, I have finished the race. I have kept the faith.

The Blindfold Parable (Part 2) Testing Faith

Thomas:
(smiles to himself and looks at seeds)

Narrator:
Thomas holds up the remaining mustard seeds, literally cool enough to wonder if he'll ever need the 4 Leaf Clover cream again. Perhaps Faith knew was she was doing after all, though Thomas couldn't determine how. As he keeps pondering how, his phone begins to ring.

[PHONE RING]

Thomas:
Hello?

(Phone Voice):
Good afternoon! I'm Katelyn with the *Good News Team*, preparing you in advance that we'll be doing a story on the miracle in your town. Did you by chance witness any of while it was happening? Could we interview you?

Thomas:
I did not witness it. But I think I know how it happened! Please come over.

Narrator:
Moments later the doorbell rings.

Thomas:
Coming!

(puts on a tie and walks slowly to his front door as the Narrator)

Narrator:
He tried calling Faith, but couldn't reach her. He retrieves the business card that started it all. And as he arrives, he opens his door to another memory.

Thomas:
(opens his door and become surprised)

Oh…Lady Luck.

Lady Luck:
(stands at the door, pets with her rabbit's foot, and appears angry)

Thomas:
I didn't know you made house calls! I appreciate it and hey… nice rabbit's foot you got there. But right now's not a good t… (I Corinthians 16:13)

Lady Luck:
(interrupts)

She's not a *real* doctor, Thomas! Faith is a fraud.

Thomas:
How did you know that…

Lady Luck:
I *saw* you go in her office, okay.

(continues massaging rabbit's foot)

Luckily, I was 'at the right place at the right time,' Thomas. I came to take you back to *The Lucky Ones Clinic* and hopefully undo whatever Faith did.

Thomas:

Are you kidding? With all due respect, the way Faith works is more effective (Ephesians 6:16). Before I even knew this mountain was moved, I rested better. I didn't just sit still and let everyone 'rub it in,' I finally got up (James 1:3)! I walked with Faith (II Corinthians 5:7).

Lady Luck:

And when you walked with Faith…. I bet you were blindfolded.

Thomas:

(becomes curious)

I was! Why?

Lady Luck:

Well…

(pulls out a picture)

…let me show what you didn't see as you walked blindly with Faith, in another room, increasing your speed.

(hands him the picture)

Narrator:
Lady Luck hands Thomas a picture of him blindfolded at Faith's office, on a treadmill.

Thomas:
How can this be real?

Lady Luck:
I told you she's a con-artist! Why is this so... oh I see! You thought Faith moved this mountain?

(laughs)

Thomas:
(appears embarrassed and confused)

Narrator:
Laughter increases in Lady Luck, as Thomas sees the *Good News Team* arriving for an interview.

Lady Luck:
(stops laughing and strongly grabs Thomas's arm)

Hey... this town's not big enough for two doctors. So if you even mention Faith to them, I'll embarrass you with these pictures and your gullible story.

Narrator:
Thomas runs emotionally past everyone and into his car, to everyone's surprise (I Peter 5:9).

Thomas:
(gets in his car and drives away)

Narrator:
Driving off quickly, he can still feel the laugher from Lady Luck and all who she might tell. Once again, Thomas retrieves the business card and drives even more intently than before.

Thomas:
(arrives at the doctor's clinic and appears in a hurry to the doctor's office)

Narrator:
Walking past the secretary, and into Faith's procedure room, Thomas looks around to see a true account of a treadmill.

Doctor Powers:
(walks inside)

Thomas? Hi! Is everything okay?

Thomas:
How could you play with my feelings like this?

Doctor Powers:
What are you talking about?

Thomas:
I *trusted* you!

Doctor Powers:

Yeah... and you're condition has improved, Thomas! You are making a... 'molehill out of a mountain' (I Thessalonians 3:7)!

Thomas:

So... it's true? You moved that mountain? How? And why did you need me to embarrass myself by moving around on a treadmill?

Doctor Powers:

Well ... let me show you.

(pulls out the familiar blindfold)

Perception contaminates the procedure! The challenge is not me shielding this place from you; it is me shielding you from *THIS* place. You don't need thick-skin when you're not exposed.

Thomas:

(head nods and continues to listen)

Doctor Powers:

And as for the physical therapy? Well... we had to get your heart pumping (I Corinthians 2:5), at least enough to move past your 'doubting, Thomas!' And we had to work together. Remember when I told you this is a team effort? We needed each other's energy (Ephesians 2:8). And apparently it was enough for you to work with!"

Thomas:
What do you mean by… 'enough for me to work with?'

Doctor:
Oh ye of little faith (smiles). I didn't move that mountain.
YOU did! (I John 5:4)

The End

Moral
Faith is a biblically-approved, blindfolded journey within
the spiritual rights we have as God's children. And the
celebration belongs to the "team effort" between the grace
of God and the willingness of Christians to walk with it.
Faith is a process too amazing to be confused with (lady)
luck.

Share Your Thoughts
Is this parable your favorite?
Vote on our site!

Story Symbolism
- Lady Luck = Superstitions, Myths
- The Clinic = Challenges
- Dr. Faith Powers = Faith
- (Doubting) Thomas = Mankind
- Business Card = Change
- Map = Mind State
- Prescriptions = Insistence
- Desert = Deserted Place
- Christian = Fellowship
- Skin = Potential
- Sunlight = Exposure to Doubt
- Physical Therapy = Action
- Treadmill = Obstacles
- *Good News Team* = Joyful Testimony

Fun Facts
- The words "doubting" and "Thomas" appear together toward the story's end, mentioning the disciple "Doubting Thomas."
- The mustard seeds left by Dr. Faith attribute the biblical process (Matthew 17:20)
- The doctor's full name (Faith Powers) is designed like an incomplete sentence. It is "a team effort" with mankind.
- Lady Luck had her "practice" as a doctor in the desert (deserted place) where Thomas lived.
- As Thomas explained his predicament to Faith, his statement that he couldn't afford to "move" is a double meaning.
- When Faith said that "someone" was "really laying it on thick," she never said who!

Discussion Questions

1. How did you (or your listeners) feel when the picture of the treadmill was revealed? Share a story of your own when your faith was tested.
2. Why do you suppose Lady Luck followed her doubts in Faith with a threat to embarrass Thomas if he mentioned her to others? Did Lady Luck seem more jealous or afraid of Faith?
3. When Faith said that "someone" was "really laying it on thick," she never said who! How likely is it that she was talking about Thomas? Share your thoughts.

Instant Replay Bible Study

Scripture Index

I Corinthians 16:13

Watch, stand fast in the faith, be brave, be strong.

Ephesians 6:16

Above all, taking the shield of faith with which you will be able to quench all the fiery darts of the wicked one.

James 1:3

Knowing that the testing of your faith produces patience.

II Corinthians 5:7

For we walk by faith, not by sight.

I Peter 5:9

Resist him, steadfast in the faith, knowing that the same sufferings are experienced by your brotherhood in the world.

I Thessalonians 3:7

Therefore, brethren, in all our affliction and distress we were comforted concerning you by your faith.

I Corinthians 2:5

That your faith should not be in the wisdom of men but in the power of God.

Ephesians 2:8

For by grace you have been saved through faith, and that not of yourselves; it is the gift of God.

I John 5:4

For whatever is born of God overcomes the world. And this is the victory that has overcome the world: our faith.

Chapter 4

Experience The Characters!

- A non-fictional experience!
- Read their Essays
- Take their Challenges

Frank & Christian
From *The Thirsty Cup Parable*

The good news, for both Christian and Frank, is the sound of their much taller friend walking down that same hall. And that person is you! Can you them fill their cup? Can you store 20 scriptures by taking *Christian's Challenge.*

Here's how: Visit *www.ChristianParables.com* and print a free bible trivia copy of *Christian's Challenge.* Good luck!

The Detective
From *The Lawyer's Lullaby Parable*

What kind of skills would a detective need to have to investigate without any details, like this one? Read the Detective's *Charity versus Ability* essay and "discover" 3 essential things to be effective in any "case!" Page 225

Corey and Jeffrey
From *The Batteries Not Included Parable*

Take their *Stay Connected Challenge*
- Write down a "cordless" moment of your own and why.
- Write down some unique gifts that God has given you.
- Ask a friend "to be your Corey," ensuring that "both increase in value" over time.

The Waitress
From *The Waitress's Tip Parable*

She's ready to 'dish about those dishes!' After all, the Waitress no longer works for them anymore, right? As she continues hiding around to warn more customers, you have a unique opportunity to help her spread this fulfilling message further! Read and share her rhyming mission as a *Camouflaged Prophet*. (Page 230) God bless!

The Other School Boy
From *The Counselor's Gift Parable*

No one got the other side, hearing from the other boy: the real Honor Student. But you can! Read his essay *The Top 20 Biblical Signs of a Fool* on Page 231.

The Celebrity
From *The Calendar's Watch Parable*

The story never actually mentioned actually was The Celebratory is famous for! The Celebratory was a musical communicator (Rapper). But now, with her new endorsement deal, she is a new and improved Christian Rapper. Experience her uplifting lyrics in *Perception Bearer*. (Page 234) Have fun!

Charity versus Ability

You've heard it before: "Give a man fish and you'll feed him for a day. But teach him how to fish and you'll feed him for a lifetime."

We can *simplify* this saying to "charity versus ability." And ability wins every time in every area, even spiritually! Tell me something: do you believe the biblical equivalent of this motto has a preference between the two:

"Give a man a fish (isolated blessing)."
"Teach us how to fish (make your own anointed way)."

Nobody's trying to "rock the boat" with a control-taking philosophy that sounds "fishy." These scriptures speak for themselves with a clear preference (Genesis 1:26-31, Psalms 82:6). And it's agreeable. Receiving charity (fish) is not bad! But the original, CEO of the earth, who shares God's image is worthy of the latter: to learn how to fish (create their own anointed way). All too often, Christians are spiritual doormats with their God-given authority. And it's about as logical as price-bargaining for last year's calendar: worthless and outdated. These are New Testament times my friend! So get your fishing pole out. And prepare to "rill in" the tools to do-it-yourself (Ecclesiastes 2:26).

1st Tool: Wisdom

In the Bible wisdom is depicted as a woman, holding riches and honor in her left hand, and long life in her right (Proverbs 3:15). Apparently Solomon was already smart for choosing the "tool (wisdom)" over an isolated piece of salmon (charity) (II Chronicles 1:10). As result, he ended up with the whole blessing combo: riches, honor, and long life (II Chronicles 1:11-12). Mathematically, [Seek Ye First = Wisdom].

Or maybe you should just wait on the Lord (for charity)? Consider this: the word "patient" is found in the Bible only nine (9) times. And three (3) of those times pertain to the rapture. A few others celebrate the Holy Spirit and a good wife. So really, the patient concept shines only 3 times. On the other hand, would you care to guess how many times the word "wisdom" can be found? It's two hundred twenty-two (222) times. That might give your blessing needs a little more perspective.

So how do we get this tool? Simply, and faithfully, just ask God (James 1:5) (Proverbs 2:3-6). And when we completely possess this "tool," then seeking financial or medical "fish," if you will, wouldn't be necessary. We can create it through wisdom.

2nd Tool: Knowledge
I believe we've "hooked" Hosea 4:6. Rill it in please! And as you do, let's address the difference between wisdom and knowledge? How are they not the same? Well, wisdom is like a coach celebrating with it's player (knowledge) after winning the championship! So now we're getting to the labor part of decision-making. Knowledge is a hands-on, informative, scavenger hunt for betterment.

Now it's important to recognize God's personality in this scripture (Hosea 4:6). God actually takes the rejection of knowledge so *personally*, that He promises to opt out of your issue Himself! And what's worse, is you're fired by even the thought of priesthood or grooming. Maybe that's why "many are called. Few are chosen." It's not a Heaven lottery which places our effective church leaders! Instead, it's the attitude towards acquiring knowledge.

But where does knowledge come from? Would you believe me if I said Knowledge comes from (a specific) fear? See for yourself (Proverbs 1:7). That's right! "The fear of the Lord is the beginning of knowledge." Specifically, fear and reverence are synonymous. Tell me how can you completely obey what you don't completely fear? And how then can we expect complete knowledge, which is useful for complete wisdom, which results in complete blessings? Most Christians fail right here. God is slighted right here. Many so-called, tribulation-claiming, Christians are guilty of a paradox:

- Late to (an effective) church (when they come). But they have perfect attendance at their job.
- Finally worked up the nerve to invite the beautiful girl downstairs. But they only "flirt" with *The Man Upstairs*.
- Will cram all night for a college exam. But they haven't studied their own heart for decades.
- Will sacrifice their comfort to a slot machine. But they treat faith more like a hobby.
- Know the HTML codes to link their pictures. But they think "Habakkuk" is a typo right now (it's a book in the Bible).
- Tune into a celebrity's interview thoroughly. Yet, they haven't read God's emotional tell-all interview in Jeremiah.

Who are these people fooling? Do they think the Gospel is a chain-letter? A diet, maybe? Or is it as easy as lukewarm passion being in denial? Welcome to the consequence of invisible question marks.

Here's the equation: [Fear of the Lord = Knowledge]. Knowledge isn't only power. It's also a protector (Ecclesiastes 7:12). Do you "know" what happens to men who love pleasure (Proverbs 21:17), who ignore discipline (Proverbs 13:18), men who possess waywardness and complacency? (Proverbs 1:32) Knowledge is the biggest shortcut you can ever employ in your life. So get all you can (Proverbs 10:14).

3rd Tool: Joy

Many people use this term too loosely nowadays. Real joy is a gift that can only be given from God. In Proverbs 15:15: "All the days of the afflicted are bad, but a cheerful heart (or joy) is a continual feast." This is why so much worldly surveillance follows them. We're talking about a heavenly imported emotion. Add to that, it can't be cloned, interrupted (without permission), or sold. And with this download from the Holy Spirit, we epitomize the mystery, the envied target of anyone currently outside our inside experience. All the mocking, scoffing, competition, strife, and plotting (Psalms 35:20-21) are merely "fruits" of an unattainable desire (Galatians 5:22-23).

So what is the artificial alternative to joy? It's called satisfaction. And it doesn't last. Experiences from drugs, riches, and all fleshly pleasures expire. Many of them only last for seconds. But joy, just like love and every other touch from God, lasts forever. How many of us remember the children's church song entitled, "Joy-joy-joy?" Later on, it lyrics "...down in my heart [your possession] to "stay" [forever]." If you live your life without real joy from our God, you'll never get past your spiritual craving for happiness. You'll live your whole life only negotiating with your heart's hunger, and never truly stopping it (II Peter 2:9-10).

The Lord used the same tools to create the world (Proverbs 3:19-20). Surely we can establish our path and lives, to a certain extent! I believe that man's dominion is overlooked during prayer because of God's eternal mindfulness. But how can our "cup runneth over" if we drink straight from the faucet?

It's not an issue of pride to enforce our "dominion." I'm inclined to believe God enjoys hearing "I got this" from a confident, anointed, spiritually independent believer. So instead of waiting for a single "fish," let us become fishers of dominion and eventually, fishers of men (Matthew 4:19).

Camouflaged Prophet

Allow me to explain how I became a success,
making history by the very essence you test
I spell victory: "J-E-S-U-S"
And I confess that He's the best,
while trying to rescue the rest
Underestimated? Yes. But dedicated no less
I'm in this war, secretly, like "checkmates" in chess.
I make Satan stress. I camouflage the way that I dress
so I can speak to other people and ... save 'em from death.

Imagine "truth" enact a new earth form
II Timothy mentions me in Chapter Two, Verse Four:
a peaceful soldier with an attitude that thirsts for war,
and gratitude to the Lord as I've first explored HIS face!
With enough faith to make a curse break,
I've been the devil's worst fate since my birthdate:
a *Camouflaged Prophet*,
making the mockers run by plottin' on the rotten
who've forgotten the "Begotten Son." And it's fun!

Let's come with verses, for every person surfacin' curses,
allergic to church services, yet swear that they're perfect
because the circus, that they call "their life"
of searchin' for purpose is worthless
and dissolves in strife.
My excursion is this:
making my essence my art, testin' hearts
When I arrive creating question marks,
they're destined to start... thinking
and won't recognize my best disguise
for stressing these lessons of mine.
So my faith is not blinking!

The Top 20 Biblical Signs of a Fool

Which would you prefer?

- to bear someone's foolishness?
- to be foolishly in front of a bear?

Well King Solomon had a louder scream for one (Proverbs 17:12). And wisdom agrees that the real stampede belongs in our civilized society! No rain forest or jungle can hold a candle to a fool in their natural habitat. And here's why:

A fool speaks like an alcoholic drives (Proverbs 17:7), crashing into conversations with their tongue running down every "yield" or "stop" sign on the road to *Their Way* (or *The Highway*) with no "coverage." Be their passenger if you dare. Feel the emotional hit-and-runs. Peek at the absolutely "totaled" relationships in their rear view mirror. And bond with your seat belt. Do these fools ever check their "blind spot?" Do they ever signal? And is a fool simply "under the influence?" Unfortunately it's much more deliberate than that my friends. It's more of a purpose than an "accident." Let's pull them over through scripture.

The Top 20 (Biblical) Signs of a Fool: hands folded (Ecclesiastes 4:5 & Ecclesiastes 10:12), self-medicating laughter (Ecclesiastes 7:6), and a boycott on what's reasonable. Silence is their only camouflage (Proverbs 17:28). Always standing up for their downfall, fools insult hope and stumbling off the same obstacles all their life (Proverbs 4:19). A true fool only flirts with imported thoughts to support their addiction to ignorance (Proverbs 18:2). Picture their restraining order on knowledge (Proverbs 1:7) and imagine diplomacy itself as their bodyguard. Yet they're only spiritually unapproachable. You can catch these characters with an economic entourage of designated thinkers. It's a self-racketeering experience (Proverbs 26:3)! But, they're just too patronized to see this.

Fools can't even secretly blend in with the more innocent of social offenders (personality disorder sufferers)! Whoever has ears, let them hear a slight accent in their accountability, meaning that their apologies sound more like an offer to tutor the offended on their ethical mystery (where they have seniority). And there's no riddle to their anger that's so easy to see (Proverbs 12:16) when it doesn't work. Not even a psychologist could intervene without scripture. But a fool's equation all 'adds up' in the Bible.

Fools want to camouflage their intimidation. It's a Cain-and-Abel relationship with wisdom itself: they secretly know their sacrifices aren't enough and clash with God's favor. So the misplaced anger becomes that foolish environment which outperforms an angry bear (Proverbs 17:12). Behold another (self-made) angry earth customer (Proverbs 19:3). Wisdom finds it difficult to pity the fool.

"Lions and tigers and *fools*... oh *my!*" Follow the yellow-*heart*-road to this wilderness of existence. Forget that bear! Observe a fool building a dam with an actual "damn!" Watch them swing like monkeys on vines of intoxication (Proverbs 20:1). But beyond the spiritual dam they've built, where nothing gets through, what's even scarier is their tendency to hallucinate even when sober (Galatians 6:3)! In the school of life, these class clowns never understand that they themselves are the real entertainment! As they are blindfolded by their ego (Ecclesiastes 2:14), campaigning for their own downfall (Proverbs 18:6), you can't help but laugh. But if their "ears that do not hear (Jeremiah 5:21)" ever decide to listen, I would tell them it doesn't have to be this way. I would echo the sound advice, "Let your laughter be turned to mourning (James 4:9) (Ecclesiastes 2:2)," give your perception a proper burial (I Corinthians 5:13), and finally live the life God has in store for you. Until then, I present to you the *Top 20 Biblical Signs of a Fool.*

Perception Bearer

As a "Perception Bearer,"
I'll re-direct this deception era so fearless
with lyrics much like reflections of a mirror to spirits:
They'll see themselves as He prevails
I'll have 'em catching your errors and dodging hell
The devil see's *me* as a weapon of terror!

I watch 'em understand those underhanded
tactics of Satan
I'm rarely trapped in this wonderland
to practice my waitin'
for folks to cease the lies and rumors and repent
before these "Delilah-juniors" get the hint of their strength
and commence.

There's nothing done in vain
No fun and games. I'm runnin' thangs
I aim the scriptures like a loaded gun....then BANG,
invading evil with anticipation
'cause *that's* what "black and white and red all over..."
... this nation (filled with hatred).
It's not a "newspaper!" It's me and you neighbor,
until we work to convert these fools that hate us
with attitudes that make us grieve
But believe I'm healing some
and won't leave 'til God's Will be done!

My essence won't expire until you understand His ways!
And people think that I've retired as a "Lamb of Praise"
But I'll never switch up.
So let the hypocrites call me silly
though I'm richer in scriptures ...

It's really just a game of *hide-and-seek*
when you're wise and meek.
As a modern day disciple, I'll disguise my reach
so when I teach, I will always reach ya'
A camouflaged preacher that's turning out New Creatures
screaming, "Satan I beat ya!"

NEW CHRISTIAN PARABLES

Share Your Thoughts!

We'd love to hear from you! Honest book reviews are greatly appreciated! Tell us a few things:

- Which parable was your favorite?
- Did you enjoy finding the scriptures before, after, or during the new parable? Why?
- How smooth of a transition is this style for traditional bible study?
- Does *WordPlay Christian Parables 2* live up to the original *WordPlay Christian Parables 1* in the series?

To review, visit our site at *www.ChristianParables.com* to find your retail link. We thank you in advance. God Bless You!

Acts 20:24

But none of these things move me; nor do I count my life dear to myself, so that I may finish my race with joy, and the ministry which I received from the Lord Jesus, to testify to the gospel of the grace of God.

Acts 26:18

To open their eyes, in order to turn them from darkness to light, and from the power of Satan to God, that they may receive forgiveness of sins and an inheritance among those who are sanctified by faith in Me.

I Corinthians 2:5

That your faith should not be in the wisdom of men but in the power of God.

I Corinthians 2:8

Which none of the rulers of this age knew; for had they known, they would not have crucified the Lord of glory.

I Corinthians 2:13

These things we also speak, not in words which man's wisdom teaches but which the Holy Spirit teaches, comparing spiritual things with spiritual.

I Corinthians 5:13
But those who are outside God judges. Therefore "put away from yourselves the evil person."

I Corinthians 6:19
Or do you not know that your body is the temple of the Holy Spirit who is in you, whom you have from God, and you are not your own?

I Corinthians 7:23
You were bought at a price; do not become slaves of men.

I Corinthians 9:24
Do you not know that those who run in a race all run, but one receives the prize? Run in such a way that you may obtain it.

I Corinthians 9:25
And everyone who competes for the prize is temperate in all things. Now they do it to obtain a perishable crown, but we for an imperishable crown.

I Corinthians 9:26
Therefore I run thus: not with uncertainty. Thus I fight: not as one who beats the air.

I Corinthians 12:4
There are diversities of gifts, but the same Spirit.

I Corinthians 12:8
For to one is given the word of wisdom through the Spirit, to another the word of knowledge through the same Spirit.

I Corinthians 12:27

Now you are the body of Christ, and members individually.

I Corinthians 13:4

Love suffers long and is kind; love does not envy; love does not parade itself, is not puffed up.

I Corinthians 16:13

Watch, stand fast in the faith, be brave, be strong.

II Corinthians 1:6

Now if we are afflicted, it is for your consolation and salvation, which is effective for enduring the same sufferings which we also suffer. Or if we are comforted, it is for your consolation and salvation.

II Chronicles 1:10

"Now give me wisdom and knowledge, that I may go out and come in before this people; for who can judge this great people of Yours?"

II Chronicles 1:11-12

Then God said to Solomon: "Because this was in your heart, and you have not asked riches or wealth or honor or the life of your enemies, nor have you asked long life - but have asked wisdom and knowledge for yourself, that you may judge My people over whom I have made you king - wisdom and knowledge are granted to you; and I will give you riches and wealth and honor, such as none of the kings have had who were before you, nor shall any after you have the like."

II Corinthians 1:24

Not that we have dominion over your faith, but are fellow workers for your joy; for by faith you stand.

II Corinthians 2:11

Lest Satan should take advantage of us; for we are not ignorant of his devices.

II Corinthians 3:17

Now the Lord is the Spirit; and where the Spirit of the Lord is, there is liberty.

II Corinthians 4:4

Whose minds the god of this age has blinded, who do not believe, lest the light of the gospel of the glory of Christ, who is the image of God, should shine on them.

II Corinthians 5:5

Now He who has prepared us for this very thing is God, who also has given us the Spirit as a guarantee.

II Corinthians 5:7

For we walk by faith, not by sight.

II Peter 2:9-10

Then the Lord knows how to deliver the godly out of temptations and to reserve the unjust under punishment for the day of judgment, and especially those who walk according to the flesh in the lust of uncleanness and despise authority. They are presumptuous, self-willed. They are not afraid to speak evil of dignitaries.

Daniel 11:35

And some of those of understanding shall fall, to refine them, purify them, and make them white, until the time of the end; because it is still for the appointed time.

Deuteronomy 11:18

Therefore you shall lay up these words of mine in your heart and in your soul, and bind them as a sign on your hand, and they shall be as frontlets between your eyes.

Deuteronomy 29:29

The *secret* things belong to the LORD our God, but those things which are revealed belong to us and to our children forever, that we may do all the words of this law.

Ecclesiastes 2:14

The wise man's eyes are in his head,
But the fool walks in darkness.
Yet I myself perceived
That the same event happens to them all.

Ecclesiastics 2:17

Therefore I hated life because the work that was done under the sun was distressing to me, for all is vanity and grasping for the wind.

Ecclesiastes 2:2

I said of laughter "Madness!"; and of mirth, "What does it accomplish?"

Ecclesiastes 2:26

For God gives wisdom and knowledge and joy to a man who is good in His sight; but to the sinner He gives the work of gathering and collecting, that he may give to him who is good before God. This also is vanity and grasping for the wind.

Ecclesiastes 4:5

The fool folds his hands
And consumes his own flesh.

Ecclesiastes 7:6

For like the crackling of thorns under a pot,
So is the laughter of the fool.
This also is vanity.

Ecclesiastes 7:12

For wisdom is a defense as money is a defense,
But the excellence of knowledge is that wisdom gives life to those who have it.

Ecclesiastics 7:25

I applied my heart to know, to search and seek out wisdom and the reason of things, to know the wickedness of folly, even of foolishness and madness.

Ecclesiastics 9:16

Wisdom is better than strength. Nevertheless the poor man's wisdom is despised. And his words are not heard.

Ecclesiastes 10:12

The words of a wise man's mouth are gracious,
But the lips of a fool shall swallow him up.

Ecclesiastics 12:1

Remember now your Creator in the days of your youth,
before the difficult days come, and the years draw near
when you say, "I have no pleasure in them:"

Ephesians 1:13

In Him you also trusted, after you heard the word of truth,
the gospel of your salvation; in whom also, having
believed, you were sealed with the Holy Spirit of promise.

Ephesians 1:17

That the God of our Lord Jesus Christ, the Father of glory,
may give to you the spirit of wisdom and revelation in the
knowledge of Him.

Ephesians 2:8

For by grace you have been saved through faith, and that
not of yourselves; it is the gift of God.

Ephesians 4:30

And do not grieve the Holy Spirit of God, by whom you
were sealed for the day of redemption.

Ephesians 6:13

Therefore take up the whole armor of God, that you may be
able to withstand in the evil day, and having done all, to
stand.

Ephesians 6:16
Above all, taking the shield of faith with which you will be able to quench all the fiery darts of the wicked one.

Exodus 20:18-19
Now all the people witnessed the thundering, the lightning flashes, the sound of the trumpet, and the mountain smoking; and when the people saw it, they trembled and stood afar off. Then they said to Moses, "You speak with us, and we will hear; but let not God speak with us…"

Exodus 20:20
And Moses said to the people, "Do not fear; for God has come to test you, and that His fear may be before you, so that you may not sin."

Exodus 20:21
So the people stood afar off, but Moses drew near the thick darkness where God was.

Exodus 20:22
Then the LORD said to Moses, "Thus you shall say to the children of Israel: 'You have seen that I have talked with you from heaven.

Galatians 2:2
And I went up by revelation, and communicated to them that gospel which I preach among the Gentiles, but privately to those who were of reputation, lest by any means I might run, or had run, in vain.

Galatians 3:24

Therefore the law was our tutor to bring us to Christ, that we might be justified by faith.

Galatians 5:22-23

But the fruit of the Spirit is love, joy, peace, longsuffering, kindness, goodness, faithfulness, gentleness, self-control. Against such there is no law.

Galatians 6:3

For if anyone thinks himself to be something, when he is nothing, he deceives himself.

Genesis 1:26

Then God said, "Let Us make man in Our image, according to Our likeness; let them have dominion over the fish of the sea, over the birds of the air, and over the cattle, over all the earth and over every creeping thing that creeps on the earth."

Genesis 6:5

Then the LORD saw that the wickedness of man was great in the earth, and that every intent of the thoughts of his heart was only evil continually.

Hebrews 11:1

Now faith is the substance of things hoped for, the evidence of things not seen.

Hebrews 11:6

But without faith it is impossible to please Him, for he who comes to God must believe that He is, and that He is a rewarder of those who diligently seek Him.

Hebrews 12:1

Therefore we also, since we are surrounded by so great a cloud of witnesses, let us lay aside every weight, and the sin which so easily ensnares us, and let us run with endurance the race that is set before us.

Hosea 4:6

My people are destroyed for lack of knowledge.
Because you have rejected knowledge,
I also will reject you from being priest for Me;
Because you have forgotten the law of your God,
I also will forget your children.

Isaiah 3:9

The look on their countenance witnesses against them, and they declare their sin as Sodom. They do not hide it. Woe to their soul! For they have brought evil upon themselves.

Isaiah 5:20

Woe to those who call evil good, and good evil; who put darkness for light, and light for darkness; who put bitter for sweet, and sweet for bitter!

Isaiah 11:2

The Spirit of the LORD shall rest upon Him. The Spirit of wisdom and understanding, the Spirit of counsel and might, the Spirit of knowledge and of the fear of the LORD.

Isaiah 29:15

Woe to those who seek deep to hide their counsel far from the LORD, and their works are in the dark. They say, "Who sees us?" and, "Who knows us?"

Isaiah 29:19

The humble also shall increase their joy in the LORD, and the poor among men shall rejoice in the Holy One of Israel.

Isaiah 35:8

A highway shall be there, and a road. And it shall be called the Highway of Holiness. The unclean shall not pass over it, but it shall be for others. Whoever walks the road, although a fool, shall not go astray.

Isaiah 42:20

Seeing many things, but you do not observe; opening the ears, but he does not hear.

Isaiah 49:4

Then I said, 'I have labored in vain, I have spent my strength for nothing and in vain. Yet surely my just reward is with the LORD. And my work with my God.'"

James 1:3

Knowing that the testing of your faith produces patience.

James 1:22

But be doers of the word, and not hearers only, deceiving yourselves.

James 1:5

If any of you lacks wisdom, let him ask of God, who gives to all liberally and without reproach, and it will be given to him.

James 4:9

Lament and mourn and weep! Let your laughter be turned to mourning and your joy to gloom.

James 4:10

Humble yourselves in the sight of the Lord, and He will lift you up.

James 5:20

Let him know that he who turns a sinner from the error of his way will save a soul from death and cover a multitude of sins.

Jeremiah 23:16

Thus says the LORD of hosts: "Do not listen to the words of the prophets who prophesy to you.
They make you worthless. They speak a vision of their own heart, not from the mouth of the LORD.

Jeremiah 29:13

And you will seek Me and find Me, when you search for Me with all your heart.

Jeremiah 5:21

'Hear this now, O foolish people,
Without understanding,
Who have eyes and see not,
And who have ears and hear not:

Job 1:7

And the LORD said to Satan, "From where do you come?"
So Satan answered the LORD and said, "From going to and
fro on the earth, and from walking back and forth on it."

I John 3:16

By this we know love, because He laid down His life for
us. And we also ought to lay down our lives for the
brethren.

I John 5:4

For whatever is born of God overcomes the world. And this
is the victory that has overcome the world: our faith.

John 2:14

And He found in the temple those who sold oxen and sheep
and doves, and the money changers doing business.

John 3:8

The wind blows where it wishes, and you hear the sound of
it, but cannot tell where it comes from and where it goes.
So is everyone who is born of the Spirit.

John 3:16

For God so loved the world that He gave His only begotten Son, that whoever believes in Him should not perish but have everlasting life.

John 6:35

And Jesus said to them, "I am the bread of life. He who comes to Me shall never hunger, and he who believes in Me shall never thirst.

John 9:39

And Jesus said, "For judgment I have come into this world, that those who do not see may see, and that those who see may be made blind."

John 10:10

The thief does not come except to steal, and to kill, and to destroy. I have come that they may have life, and that they may have it more abundantly.

John 14:15

"If you love Me, keep My commandments."

John 14:17

The Spirit of truth, whom the world cannot receive, because it neither sees Him nor knows Him; but you know Him, for He dwells with you and will be in you.

John 14:26

But the Helper, the Holy Spirit, whom the Father will send in My name, He will teach you all things, and bring to your remembrance all things that I said to you.

John 15:26

But when the Helper comes, whom I shall send to you from the Father, the Spirit of truth who proceeds from the Father, He will testify of Me.

John 16:24

Until now you have asked nothing in My name. Ask, and you will receive, that your joy may be full.

Jonah 2:7

"When my soul fainted within me, I remembered the LORD. And my prayer went up to You, into Your holy temple.

Luke 12:1

In the meantime, when an innumerable multitude of people had gathered together, so that they trampled one another, He began to say to His disciples first of all, "Beware of the leaven of the Pharisees, which is hypocrisy."

Luke 14:11

For whoever exalts himself will be humbled, and he who humbles himself will be exalted.

Luke 18:7

And shall God not avenge His own elect who cry out day and night to Him, though He bears long with them?

Malachi 2:17

You have wearied the LORD with your words. Yet you say, "In what way have we wearied Him?" In that you say, "Everyone who does evil Is good in the sight of the LORD, and He delights in them," or, "Where is the God of justice?"

Mark 1:15

…and saying, "The time is fulfilled, and the kingdom of God is at hand. Repent, and believe in the gospel."

Mark 7:21

For from within, out of the heart of men, proceed evil thoughts, adulteries, fornications, murders…

Mark 11:22

So Jesus answered and said to them, "Have faith in God.

Matthew 3:2

and saying, "Repent, for the kingdom of heaven is at hand!"

Matthew 4:4

But He answered and said, "It is written, 'Man shall not live by bread alone, but by every word that proceeds from the mouth of God.'"

Matthew 4:19

Then He said to them, "Follow Me, and I will make you fishers of men."

Matthew 6:24

No one can serve two masters; for either he will hate the one and love the other, or else he will be loyal to the one and despise the other. You cannot serve God and mammon.

Matthew 7:14

Because narrow is the gate and difficult is the way which leads to life, and there are few who find it.

Matthew 11:29

Take My yoke upon you and learn from Me, for I am gentle and lowly in heart, and you will find rest for your souls.

Matthew 13:13

Therefore I speak to them in parables, because seeing they do not see, and hearing they do not hear, nor do they understand.

Matthew 15:14

Let them alone. They are blind leaders of the blind. And if the blind leads the blind, both will fall into a ditch."

Matthew 17:20

So Jesus said to them, "Because of your unbelief; for assuredly, I say to you, if you have faith as a mustard seed, you will say to this mountain, 'Move from here to there,' and it will move; and nothing will be impossible for you.

Matthew 21:22

And whatever things you ask in prayer, believing, you will receive.

Matthew 23:13

But woe to you, scribes and Pharisees, hypocrites! For you shut up the kingdom of heaven against men; for you neither go in yourselves, nor do you allow those who are entering to go in.

Matthew 24:11

Then many false prophets will rise up and deceive many.

I Peter 1:22

Since you have purified your souls in obeying the truth through the Spirit in sincere love of the brethren, love one another fervently with a pure heart.

I Peter 4:7

But the end of all things is at hand; therefore be serious and watchful in your prayers.

I Peter 4:8

And above all things have fervent love for one another, for "love will cover a multitude of sins.

I Peter 5:8

Be sober, be vigilant; because your adversary the devil walks about like a roaring lion, seeking whom he may devour.

I Peter 5:9

Resist him, steadfast in the faith, knowing that the same sufferings are experienced by your brotherhood in the world.

Proverbs 1:7

The fear of the LORD is the beginning of knowledge,
But fools despise wisdom and instruction.

Proverbs 1:32

For the turning away of the simple will slay them,
And the complacency of fools will destroy them.

Proverbs 2:3-6

Yes, if you cry out for discernment,
And lift up your voice for understanding,
If you seek her as silver,
And search for her as for hidden treasures;
Then you will understand the fear of the LORD,
And find the knowledge of God.
For the LORD gives wisdom;
From His mouth come knowledge and understanding;

Proverbs 3:15

She is more precious than rubies,
And all the things you may desire cannot compare with her.

Proverbs 3:5

Trust in the LORD with all your heart, and lean not on your
own understanding.

Proverbs 3:6

In all your ways acknowledge Him, and He shall direct
your paths.

Proverbs 3:19-20

The LORD by wisdom founded the earth;
By understanding He established the heavens;
By His knowledge the depths were broken up,
And clouds drop down the dew.

Proverbs 4:7

Wisdom is the principal thing
Therefore get wisdom.
And in all your getting, get understanding.

Proverbs 4:19

The way of the wicked is like darkness;
They do not know what makes them stumble.

Proverbs 4:23

Keep your heart with all diligence. For out of it spring the
issues of life.

Proverbs 7:3

Bind them on your fingers; write them on the tablet of your
heart.

Proverbs 10:14

Wise people store up knowledge,
But the mouth of the foolish is near destruction.

Proverbs 12:11

He who tills his land will be satisfied with bread. But he
who follows frivolity is devoid of understanding.

Proverbs 12:16

A fool's wrath is known at once,
But a prudent man covers shame.

Proverbs 13:18

Poverty and shame will come to him who disdains
correction,
But he who regards a rebuke will be honored.

Proverbs 14:7

Go from the presence of a foolish man, when you do not
perceive in him the lips of knowledge.

Proverbs 14:8

The wisdom of the prudent is to understand his way, but the
folly of fools is deceit.

Proverbs 14:31

He who oppresses the poor reproaches his Maker. But he
who honors Him has mercy on the needy.

Proverbs 16:18

Pride goes before destruction; and a haughty spirit before a
fall.

Proverbs 16:19

Better to be of a humble spirit with the lowly, than to
divide the spoil with the proud.

Proverbs 17:7

Excellent speech is not becoming to a fool,
Much less lying lips to a prince.

Proverbs 17:12
Let a man meet a bear robbed of her cubs, rather than a fool in his folly.

Proverbs 17:15
He who justifies the wicked, and he who condemns the just, both of them alike are an abomination to the LORD.

Proverbs 17:28
Even a fool is counted wise when he holds his peace;
When he shuts his lips, he is considered perceptive.

Proverbs 18:2
A fool has no delight in understanding, but in expressing his own heart.

Proverbs 18:5
It is not good to show partiality to the wicked, Or to overthrow the righteous in judgment.

Proverbs 18:6
A fool's lips enter into contention, and his mouth calls for blows.

Proverbs 19:3
The foolishness of a man twists his way,
And his heart frets against the LORD.

Proverbs 20:1
Wine is a mocker,
Strong drink is a brawler,
And whoever is led astray by it is not wise.

Proverbs 21:2
Every way of a man is right in his own eyes,
But the LORD weighs the hearts.

Proverbs 21:17
He who loves pleasure will be a poor man;
He who loves wine and oil will not be rich.

Proverbs 24:24
He who says to the wicked, "You are righteous," him the
people will curse; Nations will abhor him.

Proverbs 26:3
A whip for the horse,
A bridle for the donkey,
And a rod for the fool's back.

Proverbs 29:9
If a wise man contends with a foolish man, whether the fool
rages or laughs, there is no peace.

Proverbs 29:10
The bloodthirsty hate the blameless. But the upright seek
his well-being.

Proverbs 29:18
Where there is no vision, the people perish: but he that
keepeth the law, happy is he.

Proverbs 30:16
Sheol, the barren womb, the earth that is not satisfied with water. And the fire never says, "Enough!"

Psalms 1:1
Blessed is the man who walks not in the counsel of the ungodly, nor stands in the path of sinners, nor sits in the seat of the scornful.

Psalms 15:1
LORD, who may abide in Your tabernacle? Who may dwell in Your holy hill?

Psalms 15:2
He who walks uprightly, and works righteousness, and speaks the truth in his heart…

Psalms 16:11
You will show me the path of life, In Your presence is fullness of joy. At Your right hand are pleasures forevermore.

Psalms 23:5
You prepare a table before me in the presence of my enemies. You anoint my head with oil; my cup runs over.

Psalms 35:20-21

For they do not speak peace,
But they devise deceitful matters
Against the quiet ones in the land.
They also opened their mouth wide against me,
And said, "Aha, aha!
Our eyes have seen it."

Psalms 77:10-11

And I said, "This is my anguish; but I will remember the years of the right hand of the Most High." I will remember the works of the LORD; Surely I will remember Your wonders of old.

Psalms 82:6

I said, "You are gods,
And all of you are children of the Most High.

Psalms 94:21

They gather together against the life of the righteous, and condemn innocent blood.

Psalms 118:8

It is better to trust in the LORD than to put confidence in man.

Psalms 118:20

This is the gate of the LORD. Through which the righteous shall enter.

Psalms 128:2

When you eat the labor of your hands, you shall be happy, and it shall be well with you.

Psalms 140:13

Surely the righteous shall give thanks to Your name; the upright shall dwell in Your presence.

Psalms 143:5

I remember the days of old; I meditate on all Your works. I muse on the work of Your hands.

Revelation 12:12

Therefore rejoice, O heavens, and you who dwell in them! Woe to the inhabitants of the earth and the sea! For the devil has come down to you, having great wrath, because he knows that he has a short time."

Romans 1:28

And even as they did not like to retain God in their knowledge, God gave them over to a debased mind, to do those things which are not fitting.

Romans 6:23

For the wages of sin is death, but the gift of God is eternal life in Christ Jesus our Lord.

Romans 8:9

But you are not in the flesh but in the Spirit, if indeed the Spirit of God dwells in you. Now if anyone does not have the Spirit of Christ, he is not His.

Romans 8:26

Likewise the Spirit also helps in our weaknesses. For we do not know what we should pray for as we ought, but the Spirit Himself makes intercession for us with groanings which cannot be uttered.

Romans 10:17

So then faith comes by hearing, and hearing by the word of God.

Romans 11:14

If by any means I may provoke to jealousy those who are my flesh and save some of them.

Romans 11:15

For if their being cast away is the reconciling of the world, what will their acceptance be but life from the dead?

Romans 12:6

Having then gifts differing according to the grace that is given to us, let us use them: if prophecy, let us prophesy in proportion to our faith.

Romans 15:13

Now may the God of hope fill you with all joy and peace in believing, that you may abound in hope by the power of the Holy Spirit.

I Thessalonians 3:7

Therefore, brethren, in all our affliction and distress we were comforted concerning you by your faith.

I Thessalonians 5:9
For God did not appoint us to wrath, but to obtain salvation through our Lord Jesus Christ.

I Thessalonians 5:14
Now we exhort you, brethren, warn those who are unruly, comfort the fainthearted, uphold the weak, be patient with all.

I Timothy 5:13
And besides they learn to be idle, wandering about from house to house, and not only idle but also gossips and busybodies, saying things which they ought not.

II Timothy 2:5
And also if anyone competes in athletics, he is not crowned unless he competes according to the rules.

II Timothy 2:10
Therefore I endure all things for the sake of the elect, that they also may obtain the salvation which is in Christ Jesus with eternal glory.

II Timothy 2:15
Be diligent to present yourself approved to God, a worker who does not need to be ashamed, rightly dividing the word of truth.

II Timothy 2:22
Flee also youthful lusts; but pursue righteousness, faith, love, peace with those who call on the Lord out of a pure heart.

II Timothy 4:7

I have fought the good fight, I have finished the race. I have kept the faith.

Titus 3:9

But avoid foolish disputes, genealogies, contentions, and strivings about the law; for they are unprofitable and useless.

Share Your Thoughts!

Tell us your favorite!

We'd love to hear from you!
Honest book reviews are greatly appreciated!

Tell us a few things:

- Which parable was your favorite?
- Did you enjoy finding the scriptures before, after, or during the new parable? Why?
- How smooth of a transition is this style for traditional bible study?
- Does *WordPlay Christian Parables 2* live up to the original *WordPlay Christian Parables 1* in the series?

To review, visit our site at *www.ChristianParables.com* to find your retail link!

God Bless You!

www.ingramcontent.com/pod-product-compliance
Lightning Source LLC
Chambersburg PA
CBHW071456170626
46811CB00007B/2600